His heart was racing, his mouth dry, and as he moved his hand burrowed into the bag and closed around the fat, taped handle of the knife. Blood pounded in his ears, and as he neared the first door the sounds of laughter grew louder.

She came out through the door, glimpsed his movement through the corner of her eye, and turned to face him. She gasped.

His hand came out of the bag.

PRISM

ANTHONY SHARPE

SWIFT

PRISM
a paperback published
by The Swift Press
PO Box 9, Chorlton,
Manchester, M21 2LQ

Printed in the UK by
The Short Run Press
Exeter

ISBN 0 9517638 0 6
A CIP catalogue record for this book is available
from The British Library.

A project such as this does not come together by itself. Heartfelt thanks are due, therefore, to all those, family and friends, contributors and patrons who, through encouragement and support, helped bring it to fruition.

So thank you....

Paul Harris, David and Susan Haykin
John McCumesky, Peter Nicolle,
Lawrence Mawn and Yvonne Forrest,
Stephen Raw, Patricia Richardson,
Tony Robbins, Ken and June Sinclair
Lesley Shackleton, Peter Spencer
Jack and Margaret Spencer.....

The author

For my parents,
who gave me everything,
and for Tavia....

Epilogue.

This was the place. This was the place. Yes, it felt right. Puzzled, he searched the headstones, feeling he knew all of the names, yet none of them.

He found a bench and, mindful of his newly healed wounds, carefully lowered himself onto it. He sat with his forearms resting along his thighs. His face was smoothed, he was calm, eyes level and thoughts on a distant plane.

It began to rain.

Falling, that had been his last recollection. Falling, and the repeated stabbing sensation in his back. Then blackness; a month like that. Frustrated and exhausted by pain and lack of sleep. Heavily sedated and amnesic he drifted in and out of a haze, unable to make sense of the images that taunted him, tumbling gyroscopically just beyond his grasp. His mind, his life, was a blank. But he did have his name, and because that name was his sole possesion he prized it.

He also had something else, but because it was an intangible it was an irritation. He recognised the symptoms, but the cause remained an infuriating enigma. The restlessness, the urge to seek and hurt, would spume and rear almost beyond control each time he fingered the business card he had found in his wallet. The once sharp edges had been rubbed soft by constant handling, and it was plain except for a scribbled telephone number on one side and a single printed word on the other.

PRISM

Prism, what it meant he had no idea. Yet his gut instincts, obviously well developed despite his vacant memory, insisted it meant something vital. He had to find it. To ease the restlessness and, perhaps, give him the answers.

He was a man used to control. He knew that much from the patient attitude he had adopted in hospital. To get well he needed to rest - so he rested.

The rain felt good. It shone on his lapels, glistened in his hair, tried to chill him and failed. He was strong. His patience had paid off. He was well again and ready to find the answers; PRISM.

Rising to his feet he turned for the cemetary gates at a leisurely stride and began.

*

1: Friends

With a wild shriek the gull dived for earth, snatched the proffered titbit and, with a lusty flapping of it's wings, struck for sky. Congreave followed it's upward progress until the glare from the sun forced him to look away.

The children, boy and girl, seven and four, giggled hysterically. Emma clapped her hands and raced up the beach towards him. "Do it again, daddy. Do it again!"

He gave her a hug. "Later, baby. Go keep an eye on Ben." Flashing him one of her brilliant, endearing smiles, she toddled after her brother.

His wife was on the spread rug, her knees drawn up, her arms loosely linked around them. When he sat beside her she returned his smile and he felt warmed inside; he had made the right decision.

"I've been thinking about what you said," he began. At once the strain shone on her face. She stared at him, hardly daring to hope. "Oh?"

"I've decided you're right. I'm going to quit. What we have, the kids, it's too valuable to miss out on. I'll tell Collins tomorrow."

With a cry of delight she embraced him tightly. "Thank you Colin. Thank you!"

She put the children to bed early, showered, then went to him in the bedroom. Their lovemaking was fiercely joyous, unreined, as if they had been long apart. He played on her with his lips until she could bear it no longer, and when he entered her they laughed in impassioned relief. Waves of pleasure silenced them as, gazes locked upon each other, they began to move together in strident rhythm. Bodies meeting and parting with drumbeat regularity until she cried out. With a final, jubilant murmur he collapsed upon her, numbed by the feeling as the tremoring within him slowly diminished.

Framing his face with her hands, she kissed his lips. "Thank you," she gasped breathlessly. "For everything."

His heart swelled with emotion. "I love you," he whispered. "I love you."

*

2:

"You can't do this, Colin." CORE Director Michael Collins remonstrated. "You can't just walk out.You have responsibilities here."

They were in the Director's office in the CORE annexe at the DI-6 building. Besides Congreave and Collins there was another in the room; Seeler. The legendary, the consummate professional. The man all others were measured by in the murky world of intelligence and counter-terrorism

Congreave was breathing heavily. He had been in Covert Resources for nine years. He had grown up there, he felt, despite being in the army for four years previously. The job had always been dangerous, but the older he got the less secure he felt. After years of surviving successfully one built up an amount of anti-chance, a debt of bad luck owing, and he had no desire to collect.

Collins looked to Seeler for support. "Tell him he can't do this."

Seeler raised an eyebrow. "A man's gotta do..."

A grateful smile broke out on Congreave's face; the big man understood.

Collins loosed a sigh of exasperation. "You two...! Okay, so you leave CORE. What will you do?"

"I don't know. I'll find something."

"Let me put it another way. What can you do?"

Congreave smirked. "Oh...freelance consultant, industrial counter-espionage, I hear Metrotel are opening a London office."

"If you're going to do that you might as well stay here."

"Then I'll get an ordinary job. I'm sure you could rig a watertight CV for me."

"I'm sure I could. But would you be happy?"

"I'll give it a shot." Congreave's expression hardened. "I'm quitting, Mike. Let's part friends."

There was a pause, then Collins appeared to relent. "Okay, you can go. But there are two ways out. Do you want to hear your options?"

Inhaling, Congreave agreed. "Go on."

"One: you can walk away. There'll be a settlement, you'll sign all the secret papers and we part as friends. Or two: you can fulfil a final obligation to the department, earn a sizeable...additional settlement, and we still part as friends. The reunion invitation stands either way."

A corner of Congreave's mouth lifted in a wry half smile. "How sizeable?"

"Thirty five thousand sound good?"

Congreave looked skeptical. Even Seeler showed surprise. Colin asked: "In addition to my pay-off? Do you have the authority to make that offer?"

"I can make the offer because that will be the amount you confiscate from the people you remove during the assignment."

"A bit unorthodox isn't it. What's the catch?"

"There is no catch. And this is not an orthodox department, as you well know."

Congreave was cautious. He knew how devious Collins could be. He knew he ought to refuse and get out while he still had his skin - he had carried out nine exterminations during his time at CORE and one more job might kill him. But he was tempted. The money would come in handy.

He took the safest route. "I'll talk to Anne." He left soon afterwards, grateful to be out of the building and into the daylight, glad to be away from the peer pressure, the need to perform well to fit in.

He would telephone his refusal - it would be far easier to break the news to Collins if he did not have to face him, or Seeler. Especially Seeler. The great man had practically reared him in the early years. He was the last person Congreave wanted to disappoint - after Anne.

He hurried home to his family, secure in the knowledge that he'd done the right thing.

Director Collins stood at his office window, staring out over the Thames, his hands linked behind his back.

"He'll telephone." Seeler assured him.

"He'll have to," Collins replied. "He's strapped for cash. Pretty desperate actually. It would be a great shame if he stayed out. He had great potential."

"Still has."

Collins shook his head. "No. Getting married and having kids was the worst thing that could have happened to him."

The big man smiled. "Not the worst thing."

*

She showed him the bank statements, the depressing list of debits, and the builder's invoices. The old house he had bought at a premium, and on a burdensome mortgage, had taken a lot of renovation, and his determination to have the best of everything had not helped. The ten thousand pound fitted kitchen, the styled bathroom with designer jacuzzi and gold trimmings, the hundreds of books bought to fill the gaping library shelves, they had all been a drain. And at the rear of the house, the pool that was intended to be a showpiece lay half finished. The bank had cut off the flow of funds.

Anne's reaction to his news came as a shock. In a surge of panic she had begun to flap, and had pulled the paperwork from a drawer. His response was anger: "I don't believe this. You pushed me to quit. Now you tell me I couldn't have picked a worse time."

"No..." she cut back. "I'm happy you're out. I just never thought you'd quit without having another job to go to. I just want you to understand our position."

"I thought we were okay." he snapped.

She sighed. Handed him an envelope. "This came today."

He read the letter, the polite invitation to pop into the bank for a 'chat'. In dismay he idly scratched his scalp. "We agreed I'd leave the money management to you."

"I know," she broke in. "But you ordered the kitchen and the pool, and that's why we're short."

"You needed a kitchen."

"Not at that price I didn't. And what about the bathroom, and the pool, and the new car? I'm not blaming you, I just want you to understand we need to plan."

The argument persisted sluggishly, for neither of them had the energy for vehemence. The sunny dream of freedom had fallen under a nightmarish cloud. He ended the evening with his head on his hands, eyes staring glassily at the tabletop, a tumbler of neat vodka at his elbow. Opposite him she sat, glum faced, hands wrapped around a mug of cocoa.

When the chill of the night had seeped through to him, and all seemed hopeless, he weakened, and told her about the offer Collins had made. The thirty five thousand.

She listened in a mood of resignation, as if the news was inevitable, all part of a plan to spoil her life. "I might have known. They'll never let you go. Not until you're burned out, or dead. We're trapped."

He tried to explain it was not like that, but the truth was that even he was not convinced; this mission was leaving a bad taste in his mouth and he hadn't even accepted it yet! "Look, Collins promised me..."

Her head snapped up. "So you're going to do it then?" The force of her anger startled him. He might fool himself, but not Anne.

The night ended as had so many before it; with she lying heartbroken, crying herself to sleep with her head buried in her pillow, and he lying dead still, pretending to be asleep, pretending not to hear.

It was easier to swallow his pride over the telephone. It had been two weeks - was the offer still good?

"You've missed the shipment I mentioned - the thirty five thousand, but we've had word another event is imminent. No mention of the amount this time. It could be more."

"Well, if you still want me, I'm in. Just tell me when and where."

"France," Collins replied. "You have a week to prepare."

3:
The outskirts of St Avold,
nine days later.

Culum Strong grumbled as he lit his last cigarette. It was cold in the small Renault van, but there was nothing he could do but sit and wait. His partner, snoozing in the rear, murmured thickly, a woman's name it sounded like, then with a curse sat up and rubbed at his eyes before spreading his arms and yawning. "What time is it, Cully?"

Culum glanced at his wrist. "A quarter to five. Not long now. Any coffee left in that flask?"

Finnbar Craig unscrewed the flask and poured out the last half cup of black coffee. He handed it to Culum in the driver's seat. "There you go," he muttered, his voice a soft brogue. He sat back against the wall of the van and drew a hefty semi-automatic pistol from inside his thick jacket. Restlessly he unloaded and loaded, then flipped the safety back and forth in a nervous routine that infected him whenever the time for action drew near.
"D'you think it'll go all right?"

"Should do," Culum replied over his shoulder. "The trial runs have gone smoothly enough. Once we get this home we'll be better equipped than ever to hammer the Brits."

"What time is it?"
"Buy yourself a watch, Finnbar."

Colin Congreave parked the rented Citroen in a clearing in the woods. He gave his partner a nudge. The man blinked a number of times, then pinched the space between his eyes until he was awake.

"I want to catch a few minutes sleep," Colin told him.

"You do a recce and spell me, okay?"
The man nodded, and without a word slipped out of the car. He vanished into the undergrowth. Colin settled back on his seat, rolled his shoulders to ease the tension, checked that his gun was to hand, then closed his eyes. He really had nothing to worry about - the Aussie hired by CORE to partner him was good. The job ought to go without a hitch. As he sank into slumber, his thoughts turned to Anne.

Ninety minutes later the Aussie woke him. "Time to go, mate. Want me to drive?"

Congreave massaged the back of his neck. "No, it's okay. It'll wake me up." Starting the engine, he jerked the Citroen into gear and steered along a winding narrow path. "Right," he said briskly, his gaze scanning for the ideal ambush spot he had decided upon earlier. "Let's go through it one more time:
The IRA has been buying arms from Bulgarian broker Omer Eof. Twice a month a red Fiat occupied by four of their gunnies drives along this road and stops at a picnic area close to the border. They rendezvous with a bakery truck coming the opposite way. The IRA people unload three or four cases from the truck, hand the driver a suitcase, then turn the Fiat around and head for Calais. You take it from here."

The Aussie nodded. "Okay, we hit them at the picnic zone. Wait for them to begin to unload, then straight into a firefight. We clear up, leaving the bodies and the weapons where they can easily be found, and get the hell out of there. It's a two minute job if we do it right."

They were parked a few yards from the picnic area, the Citroen concealed in the trees but perfectly placed for a fast exit. Weapons were loaded and checked, and they settled down to wait.

An hour passed. Traffic was light, but finally a heavy

truck - a forty footer, hauled into the picnic zone and stopped with much hissing of brakes. Two men disembarked. One hurried behind a thick trunked tree to relieve himself. The other sat on a rough bench and sucked nervously on a cigarette.

"Looks like they're waiting for something." The Aussie remarked. "Let's hope they don't scare off our people."

At the sound of a vehicle approaching, they tensed. Almost immediately a squat red Fiat 128 rounded a curve and steered into the picnic area. The truckers got to their feet, an air of anticipation about them.

The Fiat braked, the doors opened, and three men and one woman emerged. At sight of the woman Congreave let out a low whistle. "Mary Morrison," he whispered. "One of the Whitehall bombers."

"This is all wrong," the Aussie muttered, his gaze following the action. "There's been some change of plan." Watching, Congreave was forced to agree. The truckers had peeled off their overalls to reveal casual clothing underneath. Two of Morrison's companions donned the overalls, accepted the keys, and turned for the truck. Mary Morrison took a suitcase from the Fiat and handed it to one of the erstwhile truckers, and the small group begain to file into the Fiat.

"It's a bigger shipment," Congreave said. "Has to be. It's too big to be transferred, so they're taking the whole damn truck! It's already customs sealed, they'll sail through! Come on!"

The men high up in the cab were going to be a problem. While the Aussie skirted around, aiming to come up on the blind side of the truck, Congreave burst into the clearing, gun in hand. He ran for the girl - she was dangerous, but she saw him coming and shrieked a warning. Her companion, a stout man with curly red hair, delved into the Fiat for a weapon, but before he could fire it Congreave had hit the ground, rolled up onto one knee, and pumped two shells into him.

The remaining two men in the Fiat exploded into panic, fighting blindly to get out, but Morrison kept her cool and sprinted for the cover of a nearby bench. Congreave dare not let her escape. To slow her, he put a bullet into her thigh. With a cry she fell to the ground.

A brief salvo of gunfire burst from the truck. One of the men was leaning out of the window with an AK-47 in hand, the brutish rasp of it's rapid retort shredding the peaceful early morning air. But as he paused between bursts to re-adjust his aim he fell dead under a silenced hail from the Ingram in the Aussie's hands.

The truck thundered forward, forcing the Aussie to run alongside. Leaping onto the offside footplate, he finished off the driver with a burst through the window, then leapt free as the truck careered across the road and bumped to a halt against the embankment opposite.

Advancing on the Fiat, Congreave quickly finished off the occupants. That left Morrison. He turned.

The Renault was parked at a spot overlooking the picnic area, at the top of the steep, forested embankment. Culum Strong watched in horror and anger as Congreave advanced on Mary, his gun firmly gripped in one outstretched hand. He heard Mary shout a defiant obscenity, saw her reach for the small pistol she always carried in her jacket, and fall dead as Congreave shot her through the heart.

Rage began to erupt, and he would have raced down the hillside, gun blazing, had Finnbar not grasped him firmly by the arm.

"Easy, easy Cully." His friend insisted. Culum looked at him and saw the cold resolve on Finn's thin face.

"I know that bastard." Finn muttered, pointing at Congreave, far below, moving from body to body while the Aussie checked inside the Fiat.

"He's CORE, and he's feckin' dangerous. We have to be careful. Listen to me..." Culum's gaze was fixated on the scene below. Finnbar shook him roughly by the shoulder.

"Listen to me! We'll follow them, and we'll pick our moment. You'll have him, I promise you. Trust me."

Culum was panting. "Mary..." the sound came out strangled. "The bastid."

Below, the two small figures vanished into the trees. Moments later a Citroen burst from the undergrowth and took the road west. "Come on," Finn snapped. "I know a place we can intercept them."

As the Renault screeched into a tight turn under Finnbar's expert direction, Culum strained for a last look at his woman. The image of her falling back, lying there with that neat puncture in her breast, was one he knew would stay with him forever. It was all more than he could take. He squeezed the tears back inside him, clenched his fists, and muttered vengefully: "The bastid."

Bouncing dangerously, the Renault hit the road at sixty. "Come on," Culum urged. "Come on."

"Still something not right about this." The Aussie remarked uneasily. Congreave nodded agreement; his own inner alarm bells were jangling. He shot a glance at the suitcase wedged between them. It was large, and heavy, and if it contained cash there must be a great deal of the stuff. "They were sloppy, not having a larger armed prescence, and we were lucky."

A van appeared in the rear view mirror, closing at

reckless speed. Congreave's eyes narrowed. "Company. We better be ready."

The Renault homed in and sat on the tail of the Citroen. In the mirror Congreave caught a glimpse of the stony faces focusing on the back of his head.

The Aussie was becoming agitated. His gaze kept flicking from front to rear and his hands itched to be holding a weapon. "We're as open as meat on a counter. What way do you want to run this?"

Congreave had his foot hard down. The Citroen was hurtling along, and his concentration was on the road. He grimaced as he paused to think. "We could go head to head, but it would be close."

The look of urgency on the Aussie's face intensified: he wanted a decision. "I think the passenger is shaping to fire at us," he said, peering back. Culum was leaning out of his window, angling a rifle. There came a tremendous crash as the rear window blew out, wind rushed in, and flying fragments hailed. "We haven't much time!" he warned.

Congreave's face was strained. "Okay. You ready? Brace yourself. I'm going brake and swerve - NOW!"

He swung the wheel and the Citroen slewed, tyres screeching as they burned black lines across the road. To avoid a collision, Finnbar was forced to twist the wheel and swing around them. He immediately applied the brakes, shouting: "Go Culum Go!" as the Renault swerved to a halt.

Congreave hit the ground, taking refuge behind the open driver's door. Aiming at the Renault as it stopped, he blew out two of the tyres. They exploded with dull thuds. Then Culum Strong burst from the van and sprinted in a zigzag pattern for the shelter of nearby bushes. The Aussie sent a trail of silenced bullets after him, but did not score a hit. Then, as he reloaded, his head inadvertantly appeared in the open, and Finnbar blasted away the top of his skull. What remained of his head snapped back, and his twitching body tumbled to earth.

Congreave knew he was as good as lost if he stayed where he was. The two Irishmen were not amateurs and he was outgunned. With a spring he made the driver's seat, gunned the engine, and, as Finnbar and Culum emerged, running towards him, weapons blazing, he gripped the wheel, lowered his head, and pushed down his foot. The Citroen roared forward, struck the Renault a glancing blow and raced for the open road. In the rearview mirror he watched the scene recede, saw one of the men standing over the prone Australian, his hand jerking as, in frustration, he pumped bullets into the body. Then there was only clear road behind him, and he had time to become aware of just how hard he was breathing. Wiping sweat from his brow with a cuff, he quietly offered a prayer of thanks.

Wanting as great a lead as possible, he drove for four hours before taking a break. Once in Paris he dumped the Citroen and hired a small Ford. Then it was on to Calais, and the ferry to Dover.

Only then did he seek a quiet corner to examine the contents of the suitcase. Notes, bricks of them, thick bundles, bank fresh. And every one of fifty pound denomination. A rapid count told him they amounted to over two hundred thousand pounds. He gulped.

Two hundred thousand pounds!

The remainder of the journey passed in a dream. Life was suddenly good, so good. He'd made it, and survived. Now for Anne, and the kids, and freedom. Freedom!

Culum Strong and Finnbar took a scheduled flight to Dublin, from where they would make their way north using a hired car and perfect fake documents. Barely a word was exchanged on the journey. Culum sat stony faced, mind centred on one thought; revenge.

Finnbar's anger was of a different quality. When he and his friend had returned to the picnic area to salvage what they could from the truck they found the scene swarming with police. They must have been tipped off somehow.

The weapons were gone. He had lost the money. Now he must return to his Brigade Chief, and the council, with an explanation. He swallowed uncomfortably, not at all pleased at the prospect.

*

4:

Sir Alastair Watson stood with his hands linked behind his back and stared out of his seventh floor window in Century House. A career civil servant, he cut a portly figure, white haired and attired in a sober morning suit of traditional cut. He had the firm jaw and clear gaze of a much younger man, and had been quite an operator in his day - as he was wont to tell his subordinates over gin lunches.

There came a knock at the door, and Michael Collins was escorted in. Once the two men were alone Sir Alastair took to his comfortable leather chair and faced the CORE Director across the desk. "Update me on the Congreave situation, Michael."

Collins rapidly summarised, ending: "I think we've lost him. We'll have to find another way into the Irish group."

Sir Alastair scowled. "You know as well as I do that's impossible. We already know the ULC are plannng to upgrade their nuisance value on the mainland with a major campaign. We need a way into the active service unit run by Culum Strong, but as of yet we have little more to go on. We have yet to put faces to names. There simply isn't time for a gentle infiltration." He placed his clasped hands on the desk before him. "We must order him back. Force him if necessary."

He brooded for a few moments, then appeared to arrive at a decision. "Mull it over for a day or so. I'll do the same. We'll meet here the day after tomorrow to make a final decision."

Dismissed, Collins left the old man alone, once more peering out over the London streets.

Two days later Collins arrived in his office to find a confidential memo on his desk. He read it through quickly, then summoned Seeler.

"What's up?" the big man asked.

Collins gestured at the memo on his desk. "Looks like old man Watson has changed his mind about Congreave. He wants us to go ahead and penetrate an active service unit in Belfast. You want the job?"

"What happened? What made the old man change his mind?"

"According to this, a high level foreign operative engaged by the IRA has fallen into our hands. They want you to be him."

Seeler took a deep breath. "You think I can pull it off?"

"My main concern is that you may be too well known. Will you do it?"

Seeler made a face; he wasn't sure. "You know I don't like going over there. Let me have the brief, then I'll decide."

That afternoon he and Collins met in a small projection room and read through the file on the man captured by the police and held for questioning by Special Branch. His picture was flashed up on a screen. His face was rough hewn, rugged, much lined, with a round, bristled jaw, thin lips and a nose that tilted at an angle; obviously having been badly broken at some time. His hair was a mass of unruly red curls.

"Dominic McGarrigle, aged forty eight, origins in Belfast. Educated by the Provos in the late sixties when he was a teenager. He'd been a bit of a tearaway, picked up by the police on numerous occasions on assault charges. He was a particularly strong and violent individual, who was believed to be involved in numerous robberies. He always had money to spend. The Provisional IRA were interested in inducting him into the organisation, but he couldn't take orders. He preferred to work for money, when it suited him. He was believed to be fearless, and any attempt to intimidate him was met with a response of extreme violence."

"I'm surprised they let him live." remarked Seeler.

"Well, he could be useful." Collins replied. "He did some wet work over here, and then was offerred the chance to join a group travelling to Libya. He underwent training, and it's believed he handled a few assignments on a freelance basis. We're pretty sure he was the missing man in both the Red Brigades attack on the Rome station, and the Mollucan hostage week in Amsterdam. He became a trainer, and took on a few assignments just for the money. He is, by all accounts a cold man. Doesn't get attached to anyone or anything. Extremely skilled with weapons and his hands. He can kill without compunction."

"So how does he fit in with the IRA?"

"We believe Conor Black may be behind a splinter group calling itself the Ulster Liberation Council. This group is highly secretive, but we do know they want a high profile. They are not willing to exist in the political shadow of Sinn Fein. We know he believes the IRA are too soft; hitting so-called soft targets. Unlike Sinn Fein, the ULC has no recognised political wing, and therefore has no official voice. Conor Black and his ULC are going for broke. Force the British out at all costs."

"Suicide mission."

Collins shrugged. "Maybe they feel they have no option. The situation has no solution. Neither side willing to yield. So we have to do the hard thing and try to eliminate them. "What makes this so imperative?" asked the big man. Collins referred to his notes. "The RUC recently captured a group in a sweep and transported them to Castlereagh. One of the group snapped and spilled his guts for a deal. Connor Black, whether under the guise of the ULC or the Provos, has up to two thousand pounds of either Semtex or C4 stashed for an attack on London. The informant did not know what the targets are, but with all the recent disruption on the railways we have to accept that two thousand pounds of plastic has to be a serious threat. They have to be stopped. The hiring of Dominic McGarrigle is seen as the final piece of the puzzle; a man of his experience is not being hired as dressing. He's coming to do the business."

"So," Seeler asked in a resigned tone. "How do I get in?"

Collins managed a quiet sigh of relief. He had not been convinced his friend would take the job. "We have enough information about the meeting places. We ought to be able to decide on a strategy."

*

"Everything ready?" Congreave took the wicker basket from his wife and lugged it out to the car. Anne followed, an expression of total happiness on her face. He fitted the basket into the boot of the car, then turned to give her a hug. "Go get the kids. We can be at the house by four if we leave now."

He leaned into the car once more but was brought up sharply by her voice, and the sudden fear in it.
"Colin...."

He saw the shadow of fear on her face and followed her gaze. A car had arrived, unnoticed, and halted a few metres away. Michael Collins stood beside it. Slamming shut the door, he sauntered towards the Congreaves, a friendly smile on his face. "Good morning. How are you, Anne?"
She gave him a withering look. "You're not welcome here Mr Collins." she darted a frightened look at her husband.
"Don't be too long, Colin." she said, and hurried indoors.

Congreave gave an embarrassed shrug and muttered an apology, but Collins waved it aside. "Forget it. She's a good woman."
There was an uncomfortable pause. "This a social call?"

Collins smile contracted. He looked tense. "We need your help old son."
Congreave's brow creased into a frown. "Forget it." he snapped. "Thanks for dropping by but we're busy. We're moving house today." Leaning into the car, he hurled himself into a pantomine of industry.

Collins was undeterred. "I believe your new place is a lot bigger."
Congreave slowly reversed out of the car and faced him. "I suppose now you'll tell me I owe you because there was

more cash in the haul than expected."
Collins curled his lips wryly. "You had a windfall. Tax free. But now we need your help."

Congreave took a step forward, and despite the years they had spent together, despite their friendship, hostility shone through. "Go away Mike. We're through. Why don't you just cut your losses and walk away?"

"Because our information indicates that the IRA is going for the big one; a bombing campaign to dwarf anything ever done over here before. And only you have the thing we need."
Congreave was skeptical. "Come on. Are you trying to tell me that with all the talent in CORE, no one, not even Seeler, can do what you want?"

"Time is short, Colin. Our information is that the cell coming over here will be led by Culum Strong and Finnbar Craig. We don't even have photographs of them; that's how secretive they are. But you've seen them. You'd know their faces." He paused. "We have the highest sanction for this, Colin. There's an awful lot at stake."

Congreave felt, and looked, uncomfortable. He stared at Collins, willing him to back off, but the Director did not waver. At last Congreave heaved a mighty sigh. "I'm sorry, Mike. I'm not coming back." He turned away, and was halfway along the path to the house when Collins called him. Congreave turned. The Director was back at the car.

"One more thing, just a little something for you to keep in mind. The woman you took care of - Mary Morrison, she was Culum Strong's lover. They'd been together eight years and he adored her. He's sworn revenge, and our sources claim he knows your identity." His expression softened. "Be careful. Call me if you change your mind."
With that, he slid into his car and drove away.

Colin felt cold shivers ripple over him. Would it ever end, would it ever be over?

Anne came out of the house. As she studied her husband's face she felt sick with fear. That damned man! Why couldn't he stay away?

"Get the kids," Colin said in a voice hoarse with unease. "Let's move out of here once and for all."

*

5:

Seeler arrived at the cellars, the top secret high security holding facility maintained by the ministry for interrogation and special detention cases, and was admitted with the minimum of formality; his reputation, as always, preceding him. After a brief wait he was introduced to Seaton, the facility supervisor. A prissy, fastidious man, he fiddled with his spectacles while escorting Seeler to the cells below ground.

"I believe his prescence here is proving to be something of a bonus." Seaton was saying. Seeler nodded. "Yes, he could be the key we need."

Seaton's face lit up in a queasy smile. "Good timing and good fortune have a way of teaming up. Actually," he went on, "You're in luck. he's a big fellow, like yourself, and he was pretty rough when he came in. Fought like a madman. But he's fairly docile now. They all become that way after a while."

This was said through that same fixed, smarmy grin. Seaton was pleased at his own cleverness, and the power he held over the inmates.

Seeler smiled, humouring him. They halted before a door of thick steel. Seaton fitted a key into the lock and thrust open the door. A gust of warm air, fusty, and thick with stale human stink, flooded out, and Seaton turned up his nose.

Seeler entered alone and studied the large, bony framed man sprawled listlessly on the narrow bed. He was perfect, Seeler saw at once, and blessed his good luck. Taking another step he straddled the single chair parked by the bed.

The man on the bed returned the stare with eyes of pale blue. His red beard was straggly, his hair coiled and greasy, and lines of fatigue scored his face. He was close to breaking. "What d'ye want?" he croaked.

Seeler waited a moment before replying. "I want you to have the chance to get out of here."

Dominic McGarrigle attempted laughter, but collapsed into a fit of coughing. He'd led a hard life, and though he was strong his health was never perfect. With a snorting sound he cleared his throat and spat expertly into the bin by the bed. "Help me, is it?" he muttered caustically. "Now why would you want to do that?"

Seeler was calm. "Because you can help me"

A dull, grating chuckle shuffled rustily in the prisoner's throat. An avaricious glimmer shone in his eyes. "I already have a job. I'm being paid."

"You have a contract, but as we both know, it's unlikely you'll be free to collect. You're a professional. I respect that. What I'd like to do is better the offer you have been made. I'd like to hire you."

"What do I have to do?"

"Teach me to be you. I have a job to do, and to finish it I need to know everything you know. Once I've succeeded, and I'm home again, you go free. A wealthy man."

"I thought that might be the case," McGarrigle muttered. He lapsed into silence, brows knitted as he concentrated. He was not a man to give trust easily, but he recognised the futility of being imprisoned. He darted a glance at Seeler. "What guarantees do I have?"

"We can work that out."

McGarrigle rubbed at the bristles that silvered his jaw. He came to a decision. "Okay, but let me tell you. It's going to cost you - you bastard."

6:

Ever so gently, the Watcher parted the curtain of tall grasses and gazed at the house some fifty metres away. The overgrown grounds were a blessing. He would be able to make his approach unseen, and once inside.....

On his elbows he covered the ground, careful to let the yielding grasses close over and behind him to mask his progress. At one point, hearing voices, he parted the grasses once again and saw the woman - Congreave's wife, playing ball with the two kids. He waited, for the work had to be completed indoors, and as he waited he listened to the childish laughter and thought: shame about the kids...

At length, they returned indoors and he continued to drag himself to the yard where, pausing only to brush soil and traces of grass from his clothes, he rose to his full imposing height and trod quietly towards the house. He halted by the door to adjust the bag slung over his shoulder, then opened the unlocked kitchen door and stepped inside. The kitchen was in darkness, but the large windows admitted enough light for him to make out the symmetrical outlines of the furniture. He took his time; he wanted no mistakes, and waited until his eyes had fully adjusted to the gloom. Then he crossed the room and stepped into the brightly lit corridor that cut through the centre of the house. He could see doors leading into other rooms, could hear muffled laughter coming from one of them. A child's laughter.

Forcing himself to concentrate, he shut out the sound and moved silently along the corridor. His heart was racing, his mouth dry, and as he moved his hand burrowed into the bag and closed around the fat, taped handle of the weapon. Blood pounded in his ears, and as he neared the first door the sounds of laughter grew louder, rang out like the pealing of golden bells. And a maternal voice, full of love, said: "Come on, the two of you. Off to bed."

She came out of the door, glimpsed his movement through the corner of her eye, and turned to face him. She gasped.

His hand came out of the bag.

*

Jack Burt, hugely successful American commodities broker, left his newly opened London office and began the ninety minute drive to his new home. He and his family, English wife Carol and the kids, Brett and Donna, had fled the hectic confines of New York for the more sedate pace of English life. The NY office was well run and profitable, and Jack had grasped the chance to build up the London office personally.

Carol had been ecstatic at the thought of returning home, and she had found the perfect first house for them,their intended base for the next two or three years. Large and slightly rundown, but with much recent renovation, the house had four bedrooms and two bathrooms, with enough ground surrounding it to satisfy any child. Jack had been pleased with Carol's choice. He liked to get his hands dirty at weekends and there was a challenging mass of unruly grasses to be tamed. And then, there was the half-completed pool...He smiled at the prospect of finishing that project himself.

They had been in the house for less than one week but already he had memorised the route. Traffic was light, and he was making good time. Back in the States, he was never home early enough to read the bedtime stories. Now he had that pleasure, and he loved it. He felt real appreciation of the improvement in the quality of his homelife. Thinking of the kids brought a fond smile to his face. Family, you couldn't beat it.

Dusk was settling on the landscape as he sped along the unmade road leading to the house. England was great! Okay, the roads were crap, unbelievably narrow, and the streets dirty - where weren't they? But there was still a certain elegance, a certain gracefulness. How proud he had been when he told his friends back home: "We're going to live in England!"

He braked in front of the house, doused the headlamps, and let himself in through the front door. He called out: "Honey, I'm home!"

It was at that instant the nightmare began.

The house was eerily quiet, and something in the back of his mind remarked on the unusual calm. Then his gaze lit upon the smear of red paint along one wall; that was careless of the children. Careless of Carol to let it happen. There was a smell in the air. A tangy smell, a fresh smell that was infuriatingly familiar, like something he'd known years before and forgotten all about. He could not put a name to it. Then he turned into the lounge - and froze. Horror met him full-on, swamped him with almost hurricane force. Carol, his lovely wife, lay sprawled on the couch, her head lolling too far backwards.

His first thought was that someone had daubed her with red paint too, but then he recalled the smell, and memory plucked it's name from the lost file where it had lain for years and flourished it before him in triumph. It's name was blood. Spilt blood, and Carol...

"Oh God!!" he cried, dashing to her. He touched her cheek, felt it's slight warmth, then gingerly, and in horrified disbelief, ran his fingers over her. He took one of her small hands in his. Felt the sticky blood, stared at the deep black wounds, the great ruddy trails that stained her clothing.

Her throat had been cut. Not just gashed but cut. "Oh my darling, my sweet darling..." he whispered, his voice trembling in distress. Taking her head in his hands he cradled it to his chest. He hugged her tightly, and hot tears flowed, coursed down his cheeks. "What have they done to you, my love?"

He sat like that for...he had no idea how long. Then through the mist of tears he saw the wall behind the couch, the dreadful red daubing, and a new horror struck like a sledgehammer blow.

"Oh God," he breathed, gently lowering Carol's head. "Oh God..." slowly he rose to his feet. "Not the children, not the children..."

Lurching weakly along the corridor he saw more of the red daubings, the same horrific graffiti. Grasping the bannister he hurtled up the stairs and thundered into the bedrooms one at a time, shouting their names. Panic stretched taut his face, his heart pounded in his chest. Then he found them. Pathetic bloody bundles. Unrecognisable.

His heart broke. Falling upon them in a fit of uncontrollable sobbing, he hugged their small bodies in his huge embrace until he was caked with blood.

He felt trappped. Lost in some nightmarish crazy house. Before he knew it, he was roaming the house in a mindless deranged pattern, whimpering. Then slowly anger, fury overcame sorrow, and he was running through the house, up and down, screaming at the top of his voice for the killers to show themselves.

"Come out!" he shrieked hoarsely. "COME OUT!"

He tore through the building, senses reeling, nose and mouth thick with the taste and the smell of freshly spilled blood. All around him there was the sight of it, so much of it, smeared, sending him crazy with anguish. Everywhere he turned, on every wall, that word sprawled in livid, running red. Tall uneven letters, crimson, hateful, daubed in the blood of his children! One word.

MARY!

*

Jack Burt turned away from the graveside, relieved to have it behind him. Watching those caskets sink into the ground had been the hardest thing he had ever had to endure. The horrors he'd seen during two volunteer tours in Vietnam paled in comparison to the horror of burying his beloved family.

At the grave, an agonised cry broke from Carol's mother, and her knees buckled. Aided by her husband, Geoff, she was led away to a waiting car. The other mourners, mostly Carol's friends and relatives, and a small number of business aquaintances, began to file away.

Jack walked to his car and stood beside it. Tears welled, but he refused to release them. 'Not yet,' he willed himself. 'Save it for later.' Trembling, he ran a hand over his face. His skin was clammy.

Geoff was at his side, asking how he was. Jack hauled himself back on course and assured him he was fine, adding: "All things considered. How's Martha?"

Geoff glanced at the car where his wife could be seen, sobbing into a hankerchief. He swallowed. He was a proud man, and it was taking every ounce of reserve to keep him from crumbling. "I don't know if she'll ever get over it. Blast it, I know she won't." He bit his lips, blinked back tears. "She's dead inside. I've lost her too." He swayed, and almost toppled, but Jack grasped him tightly by the shoulder and willed him to be strong.

At length the older man steadied, though his hands still trembled. "Thanks Jack." he murmured. "I'm fine now. What about you, what are you going to do?"

Jack shook his head. "I don't know, Geoff. I don't want to go back to the house, and I can't return to the States until the police are convinced I'm in the clear..." He faltered. It was hard to say. To admit that he was a suspect was painful, a dreadful agony. He was still grappling with the impossible reality. He banged his fist on the roof of the car, drawing a few shy and embarrassed looks from others. "Dammit! It might help if I only knew why! What was it for? Why just rub out three lives like that? I...I..." he broke down, choking on his own tears, near strangling himself in his attempts to contain the grief.

Geoff put out a hand and said, in a soothing voice: "Let it out, Jack. Let it out. It's allowed."

At that, the damm burst, and Jack Burt, six foot three and two hundred pounds, ex All- American and former marine, fell into the embrace of a man thirty years his senior and wept like a whipped child.

*

7:
Belfast

Seeler found the place he sought - a heavily fortified, windowless building that stood like a craggy uninhabitable island on a desolate spread of wasteland near the decaying suburbs. A known but left alone drinking club, the profits from which went straight into the coffers of the Provos.

He paused just inside the door. The interior was gloomy and he wanted to give his eyes time to adjust. The furnishings were sparse - this was no nancy's bar, the few tables and chairs in evidence well used and rickety. The place buzzed with the murmur of conversation, and a dense haze of pungent cigarette smoke lined the ceiling.

Seeler made his way to the bar. He had prepared meticulously for the role by letting grow a straggly beard, dying it, and his hair, a carroty red. His clothes had all been acquired locally, and he had passed a few days listening to the locals talk, absorbing the feel of the language. The men he would be dealing with were hard, and suspicious, and if he failed to respect the conditions he would be found out - with consequences that didn't bear thinking about. His passage went unnoticed by all except the barman, a heavy jowled bruiser with a beer paunch swelling his short sleeved white T-shirt. His thick white arms were crossed, and he aimed a calculatedly hostile stare at Seeler as the big man occupied a vacant stool.

"What'll ye have?" he mumbled. Seeler wiped a sleeve across his mouth and ordered whiskey. The drink was brought with a scowl, and the money Seeler offered examined with suspicion, then the big man turned on his stool to survey the room. The barman hovered behind him; his instincts for trouble were fine-honed, and there was something about this newcomer he did not like.

"Are ye looking for somboddy?" The barman chirped. Seeler slowly turned. "Would it be any of your business if I were?" He challenged in a soft, chilling brogue. His stare was level and disturbingly calm. The barman looked into those grey eyes and saw a depth he had no desire to plunge into. Intent on saving face, he mustered a careless shrug, then turned away and made a show of collecting glasses.

Seeler smiled to himself. He had been pleased with the reaction. He cleared his throat, and hailed him: "Perhaps you can help me?"

The man grudgingly moved closer - but not too close. "Oh aye?"

"Would you know of a friendly place where a man without a place of his own can kip down, without being disturbed?"

The barman shuffled uncomfortably. "Hotels are in the city centre."

Seeler's smile was gentle. "I feel like a stranger here now. I've been away a long time. I need to reconnect myself. Find my friends again." When the barman refused to be drawn, Seeler altered tack. "Does this place ever get raided?"

"Never." The barman's scowl intensified. "We're left alone here." He grew bold behind the words, secure in the shadow of the faceless men who met in the backrooms.

Seeler leaned closer to the man, in the manner of one who imparts a secret. "I only ask because there are those looking for me who might not respect the privacy you have here."

The barman absorbed this and understood. Something uncertain flashed in his eyes, and he scuttled into a back room. Minutes later, Seeler saw him talking to a smaller individual, a man with a narrow, weasel face and darting eyes. His thinning black hair combed back, slicked with hair oil. The two men parted, the small man sauntering to

take the stool next to Seeler. Ordering a drink, he addressed the big man without looking directly at him.
"You're a stranger here?"
Seeler gave a non-committal tilt of his head. "I've been away."
"Permit me to offer you some friendly advice. This is not the sort of place where one interferes with the business of others."
Seeler turned his full gaze upon the man. "Did I say I was intending to interfere?" He noted that the man did not flinch under the stare; he was made of sterner material than the barman. Altogether different.
"Let me put it this way. We don't welcome strangers."

"I'm simply looking for a few old friends, and a safe place to lay my head."
"Believe me, there is no safety here for the curious. Take my friendly warning, find yourself a hotel in the city." The drink arrived. The small man drained his glass in a single sweep, and stalked away.

Seeler watched him leave, then ordered a refill. He sipped at it, and enjoyed the spirit burn of the liquor as it hit his stomach. At length he stood, slapped some loose change on the bar, and turned for the door.

The night was cold and he wandered like a man with no destination. Confident he had made his point, he dawdled, knowing they were watching him, knowing they would come to him once they realised he had not been frightened off. Ducking into a narrow alley he relieved himself against a wall. When he turned once more for the street it was to find his path blocked by four dark figures.

One of the figures stepped forward. "You've been making enquiries, brother." he said in a soft voice.
Seeler was ready. Breathing perfectly paced, body poised

yet relaxed. "What would that be to you?"

"This is our ground." Chipped in another of them. " If you choose to ignore our warnings we'll have to force you to leave." So saying, this man stepped forward. A club swung in an arc. Seeler moved with sure instinct; he ducked under the blow, grasped the descending forearm, and with a savage twist relieved him of the club as a second dark figure lunged. He altered his grip, and the club became a ram he jabbed into the attacker's gut. A punch was hurled at his face. Deflecting it with a raised arm, he countered, stepping through with an open-palmed blow that knocked the assailant off his feet.

The last man was wily. He had a knife and he circled, his breath coming in visible spurts of mist. He feinted, hoping to force Seeler backwards, but instead the big man stepped in, crushed the attack with a powerful downward blow and floored the man with a swipe across the face.

Standing over them, and barely out of breath, he said, in a thick accent: "My name is Dominic. If the name means nothing to ye, then you can't know much. I've been away a long time, but I'm back now, and I'm ready to dish it out until you're ready to take me to a safe place."

The wily man got to his feet and rubbed at his jaw. He looked around at his companions, sprawled on the ground, and he marvelled; they had never been taken apart like that, even singly. He looked to the big man. "Dominic, is it? How long have you been away, friend?"

"Fourteen years." Seeler answered gruffly. He affected the sheepish tone of a powerful man slightly ashamed of his strength. "I've been far away, working for the cause."

The wily man put away his knife and stepped forward, extending a hand. "We were expecting you three weeks ago. We were worried. We thought the Brits might have had you.

Welcome home. I've heard talk of you - when I was in Long Kesh. My name is Danny Magee. Come on, we have a place for you."

*

Jack Burt was packing. The house stood empty, the silence numbing as he systematically packed away his family's belongings. Every now and then he would come across some treasured item - a toy that evoked a particular memory and brought a wistful smile to his face, or one of Carol's favourite pieces. When this happened he would almost falter, but would swallow his heartbreak and force himself to continue.

The walls still shrieked red. He had not had the heart to remove the horror, even with it's awful associations. For to clean the walls would be, somehow, removing a link with the past. He looked at that dreaded word: MARY. And for the millionth time he wondered about it's significance. The minutae of his life, past and present, had been picked over with painstaking detail by the police, but he had been cleared. It was not without relief he heard this verdict, for the crime appeared to be motiveless, and he the sole beneficiary to his wife's estate.

Now, as he had been told countless times, it was time to pick up the pieces and walk on. Walk on, he muttered silently, with bitterness. Easier said than done.

Once everything of importance had been boxed, he sat

in the deserted kitchen and nursed a mug of coffee. A diary lay open at his elbow, and he stared down at the page, and the telephone number written there. He wondered if he really wanted to know, really wanted to delve that far, or if he would be wiser leaving the past alone. He ought to make the break. Come to terms with the pain and start again.

He could - if only he was able to rid himself of that damming question: Why?

Knowing he would never rest until he had the answer, he took the diary to the telephone and dialled the number.

"I know you've heard this before but, have you considered trying to put it all behind you. Going on?"

Jack sighed. He was weary of the ritual of talking, but he had to explain. "I've tried to come to terms, to rationalise, but I can't. I have to know why, what was the reason? It wasn't robbery, there was nothing taken."

The man he intended to engage read through the fat file of clippings Jack Burt had compiled. Everything written about the killings. When he had finished he gently closed the file.

Jack had a bottle of red wine open. Now he poured. "Well," he asked, "Are you interested?"

"It's an intriguing case, Mr Burt." Stanley Murdoch, ex-police officer turned private investigator commented. "But really, don't you think this would be better left to the police? They're really very good you know."

Jack took a swig of red. "They want to help but just can't commit manpower to one case indefinitely. I can't blame them, they gave it their best shot, but they have neither the motivation, nor the resources that I have. I'm the one who lost, Mr Murdoch, and I have to know why. If you'll take the case, I have the cash to see this thing through. The answer is out there somewhere. I want you to help me find it."

Murdoch took a mouthful of wine, swallowed, and grimaced. He was a beer drinker. Anything more wine-like than a Liebfraumilch sent shivers down his spine. "You know my rates?" Jack nodded. Murdoch mulled over the case; the snippets he had gleaned from the scrapbook and the pieces he recalled from the news reports. This was a strange one alright, and probably impossible too, but the American's money was as good as any, and, who knew? It might prove interesting. A case he could get his teeth into.

"Well," he said. "I suppose it will make a change from tracing errant husbands." He leaned across the table to extend his hand. "Nice to be working for you, Mr Burt. I accept."

*

9:

The barbed wire fence was down in one spot and Seeler stepped through without difficulty. The building site was deserted, just acres of half-finished dwellings, sleeping machinery and mounds of bricks and sand. He had memorised much of the layout, at least the landmarks, and found his way to the meeting point with ease. The night air was cold, and he pulled his coat tighter.

In the gloom of a near-completed house a red glow flared and diminished as his contact inhaled on a cigarette. Seeler muttered the code word and the contact, an experienced SAS officer, greeted him. "How's it going?"

Seeler accepted a cigarette. "I've made contact with the cell I was aiming for. They seem convinced of my identity."

"Are you positive?" Seeler replied that he was. He had been fully briefed on the history of the man known as Dominic, and was similar in build and height. The red hair and beard, added to the fact that no one in Northern Ireland had seen Dominic in nearly twenty years, made his task easier. "If I had to be him for too long the chances of being caught would increase; sooner or later I'd run into someone who knew him in Libya. But for the short time I'll be here I should be okay."

"So what's your next move?"

"Dominic's reputation got here before me. He's a handy fella and they won't want to waste his talents. I don't think it will be too long before they take me up a few rungs. Then with any luck I'll reach the cell leaders; Strong and Craig."

The officer nodded in satisfaction. "Sure you don't want to carry a transmitter?"

Seeler shook his head. "Can't risk it. Later maybe, when I'm better placed. Thanks anyway."

"Okay," the SAS officer murmured, stamping out the cigarette as he prepared to leave. "But remember...." he wagged a finger. "Frequent contact."

As he moved away, into the shadows, Seeler muttered: "You can count on it."

*

10:

The camp lay in the navel of the foothills. The surrounding slopes were carpeted with patchy heather, and above, the ceiling of dense cloud appeared to be suspended by the mountain tops upon which it nestled. The scene represented Scotland at it's loneliest, it's most serene, it's most magnificent.

A dozen runners, having set out four hours earlier in immaculate whites, were returning in a ragged file, muddy and bedraggled and aching, but glad they'd made the effort. As each one passed through the gate a cheer went up from those who waited, for achievement was recognised here.

Colin Congreave and his family had arrived that afternoon. Upon hearing of the killing of Jack Burt's family, he had immediately reached the conclusion the hit had been intended to hurt him. And though his heart ached with pity for Burt's misfortune, his priority had been to safeguard his own. To accomplish that, he had hastened to remotest Scotland, intent on leaving Anne and the kids in the safe keeping of one of his oldest and most trusted friends. David Parsons was tall and lean, with receding wispy hair. His complexion was ruddy, his eyes clear, with the steady gaze of a man used to seeing great distances. Now, while Anne and the kids made the most of the filling fayre served in the camp mess, he and Congreave patrolled the camp perimeter.

Parsons listened to Congreave's story and congratulated him on his decision. "They'll be safe here, Colin." he said.

They walked on, then came to a halt on the crest of a small hill. The camp was spread before them.

"You know, Dave, when you left CORE to set up this place I thought you were crazy."

Parsons smiled. "What do you think now?"
Colin gazed around at the hills and the grey-blue mountains beyond, took a deep breath of the clean air. He could almost smell the tranquillity. "I think maybe you're not so crazy. You've done well, I can see that from the size of the camp, but where does all the business come from?"

"Firstly, I keep away from Yuppies out for 'survival' weekends. We conduct a serious business here. We train key security employees; chauffeurs, bodyguards. We teach survival in the wild, what to do in hostage situations. Evasive driving etc. We also take a large number of management personnel sent here on sharpening-up exercises. They like the exclusivity, the discretion, and the quality of the training. When they leave here most of them feel like real men for the first time in years."

Colin recalled the survival courses he and Parsons had attended together years earlier, and he smiled. "Worm omelette and burnt pigeon. Perhaps I should take the course myself while I'm here."

"You should. It'll surprise you."
They walked back towards the camp. Silence settling comfortably between them. As they neared the entrance, Colin sighed. "I envy you. I really do."

"You could have been part of it." Parsons reminded him. Colin shrugged. Parsons continued: "You still could. I'm thinking of opening a second place on the continent. You'd be exactly the calibre of man I'd want to run it."

Colin said he would give the idea serious consideration. They talked about his last job for CORE, about the massacre. Parsons then asked what Colin intended doing.

"I have to look for the men who hit Burt's family. They'll know by now they missed the target and they'll want me even more. I have to get in first."

"Do you know who was behind the attack?"
Colin nodded. "A couple of hardline front-rankers in the Provos. Their names are Culum Strong and Finnbar Craig."

Parsons whislted softly. "In that case, my friend, I strongly recomend you take the course. If you're going up against them you'll need your wits about you."

Belfast.

It had been nine days since Seeler's admittance to the cell, and he was finding the prolonged deception a drain. His new colleagues had, naturally, been suspicious of him at first, forcing him to curb his impatience and concentrate on appearing relaxed; a man who had found sanctuary. Hints had been dropped, and he knew his time to be tested would not be long coming. He would have to deliver the goods if he wanted to penetrate further.

Over the nine days he had come to detest Magee. The loathsome little man could not keep his mouth shut. It was he dropping the hints - largely, Seeler suspected, in order to feed his own feelings of self importance. Through him Seeler had learned that others in the group, at a higher level, were interested in Dominic's arrival. Magee had let it be known that a little task would have to be performed before more doors would open.

He had been expecting a call, and tonight it had come. After dinner he left the safe house he was lodged at and walked the short distance to the fortress - the drinking club used by the cell leaders as a base. Taking a corner table as instructed, he nursed a double whiskey while he waited. His mind was clear, ready for anything.

When Magee arrived, Seeler had to resist the urge to

laugh. The little man had the collar of his black donkey jacket turned up, and his manner was overtly suspicious. Buying a drink at the bar he threaded his way to the table and planted himself opposite the big man.

"Hey, Dominic," he growled, gulping from his glass.

"How long do we wait?"

Danny Magee consulted his watch. "Maybe ten minutes." he took another sip. "This could be a big night for you. All you have to do is come through for these people and you're in." He aimed a playful punch at Seeler's shoulder, and the big man buried his ire behind a taut smile. Magee behaved as though Dominic were his protege, as though his patronage alone could open the doors.

Minutes later a man poked his head around the door to the street and signalled to Magee. The little man finished his drink in a single gulp, and banged down his glass. Whiskey trailed from a corner of his mouth.

"Come on," he whispered. Seeler followed him out onto the street. A dark transit van stood at the kerb, and as they passed it the rear doors swung open. Seeler and Magee climbed inside and the doors slammed shut. As he settled down in the gloom, Seeler felt his heartbeat accelerate; he had to be ready for the eventuality they had broken his cover. The engine roared, and the van swayed as it hauled away from the kerb.

Seeler's eyesight adjusted, allowing him to make out two other shapes in the rear of the van. One was Magee. The other man, squatting at Seeler's side, held out a hand. "Norm Nunney, Dominic. Pleased to know you."

"What's the crack?" Seeler asked, his soft tone like ice in the air. Already he could sense Norm's nervous awe of him. Norm explained:

"We're going to pick up a couple of fellas first. One

lives on the diamond, the other we'll pick up outside the Ardene social club. The second man is called Dessi, and he's in charge. Just a word to the wise, Dominic. Dessi doesn't take no messin'. Just do as you're told and everything will be hunky dory."

Seeler nodded, as though thankful for the advice, but internally he was jubilant. Dessi! It had to be Dessi O'Bain, one of the men most wanted by the British security forces. If Seeler could bring him in...what a coup that would be!

The pick ups were made and he shook hands with Dessi. In the half light he studied the man's coarse face; the soft jaw, the humourless lips and the dead, almost mocking eyes. The man was a killer.

Their gazes clashed. Seeler, the most proficient, most renowned assasin on earth, and the Irish freedom fighter. Now Dessi's fate was sealed. Dessi mistook the strength he saw in Dominic's slate grey eyes for kinship. He decided immediately that the big man knew his stuff.

The van was parked in a side road, and in the thin light from a battery lamp a map was opened and studied. "McGowan lives here..." Dessi indicated with a fingertip. "Number nine. We hit him, then drive to the Glenville road. A car will be waiting for us. We'll be away to lodgings near the Musgrave."

Magee asked "What do you want us to do?" His hollow face flowed with vicious eagerness in the pale light. Dessi issued orders. "Norm, you drive. I want the engine running non-stop. Did you fill her up?" Norm said he had. "Good. Now you, Magee, you knock on the door. He knows you. He'll let you in." To the fourth man, a stocky, wide-bodied man named Jimmy, he said: "You're the lookout. Anybody so much as puts a nose in our direction you let off a burst." So saying, he lifted a canvass bag he had brought with him and took out a battered machine gun. Jimmy took it, and his dull face seemed to come alive as he handled the weapon. Deftly checking it, he settled back to listen. Something in the bottom of the sack struck the floor with a heavy metallic thud as Dessi's hand rummaged.

"For you, Dominic, I have this little beauty." He brought out a semi-automatic Browning pistol and placed it in Seeler's hands. "You comfortable with it?" His gimlet gaze fixed on the big man, probing for signs of weakness.

Seeler replied that he was, then asked: "Do I need to know why we're doing this?"

Dessi frowned, and Seeler knew it had been a mistake to ask.

"No. When McGowan answers the door you force him inside. You put him on his knees in front of whatever family there is in the house, and you do the rest. Okay?"

Seeler hefted the weight. He nodded. "Okay. I know what to do."

"Good." Dessi folded the map and slotted it into his jacket. "Norm, drive us there."

The journey was undertaken in silence. Seeler had begun the relaxation process, taking slow deep breaths. He was used to killing, inurred to seeing people die because of his actions, but usually those he was paid to eliminate were scum; terrorists, drug dealers. The thought of executing a man in front of his family made him uneasy. He considered wounding the man, letting him live, but knew that if he did so the risk to himself, and to the mission, would be increased. He had to deliver the goods, or Dessi and his superiors would believe him inefficient at best, suspect at worst. Either way his penetration into the upper levels of the IRA would be halted. Clearing his mind, he waited.

The street was a poorly lit cul-de-sac that ended in a high wall. Seeler and Magee stepped out of the van and strolled at a purposeful pace towards the house. Number nine.

"You ready?" Magee hissed nervously. Seeler calmly murmured an affirmative, then stood back to let Magee pass through the gate first. Looking back, he saw that the van had turned and was gliding to a halt. He could see Norm's face, shining like a skull in the poor light as he crouched over the wheel. Next to him, Dessi sat as still as a stone, but Seeler could feel the killer's gaze upon him. Jimmy stepped from the shadows and darted a look around. The machine gun was gripped to his chest.

He heard the tremor of a doorbell as Magee jabbed the button. Seeler moved to his side. His breathing was still controlled, but his heart beat had accelerated. Light shone from indoors, and a silhouette shifted beyond the frosted glass panel in the front door. A muffled voice called out: "Who's there? Who is it?"

Magee's face was split by a toothy grin. "It's me. Danny Magee. I have to talk to you. Let me in."

"Magee? What the...?" There was a moment's hesitation, then the shadow moved and a lock turned. The door opened and McGowan came face to face with the Browning in Seeler's hand.

"Nice and quiet now." Muttered Seeler. Brushing past Magee he shepherded the hapless McGowan into the small living room.

The room was hot - a gas fire glowed bright red, and the place was littered with toys. The TV was on, volume lowered, and a half finished glass of ale sat on the arm of an easy chair. A cigarette perched on the edge of an ashtray trailed thin wisps of smoke towards the ceiling.

A woman stood at an ironing board, smoothing a shirt, and in a corner two grubby children pushed toy cars around an imaginary circuit. McGowan turned around, and Seeler saw that he was a middleaged man, balding, with a face that would have been jolly if he hadn't been terrified. His jaw hung slackly. Tears brimmed.

"Pat..." whispered the woman, the hot iron still in her grasp. She was thin, and careworn, hair hanging in lank strands. Her hollow eyes looked on with dread. "Pat, what is it? Who are these people?" But her tone betrayed the sick feeling she felt inside. She knew. The kids stared up in blank curiosity.

Magee was at Seeler's shoulder, his face eager. "On your knees, McGowan." Seeler said quietly. His control processes were clamped down tight, and the gun was gripped in a rock steady hand.

McGowan swallowed. His chest rose and fell rapidly. "Please..." he whimpered. The woman hurried around the ironing board. "No, please no. Please no..."

McGowan, coming suddenly to life, held out a hand to stall her. "No Shelagh. No. You have....you have to look after the bairns. Mister please..." he implored. "Please, not in front of the children." He swallowed, hard, and a tear strayed down a cheek. The woman looked ready to faint.

Magee swore viciously. "On your knees, McGowan!"

The condemned man continued to plead with Seeler, but the big man merely directed him with a soft voice. "On the floor. Let's get it over with."

McGowan shut his eyes tight and sank to his knees. His lips were trembling. "I love you Shelagh!" he cried. "And the kids!"

"NO!" she screamed as Seeler placed the muzzle squarely in the centre of her husband's forehead. She would have leapt upon the big man, but Magee wrapped his arms around her. "Go on," he swore as she fought like a hellcat.

The blast was of a horrific volume. The body slumped backwards, blood jetting from the wound. Standing over the twitching body, Seeler emptied the weapon into it. Then he moved for the door.

Magee released the woman. She fell upon the body, sobbing. One of the kids began to blubber. Magee stared, transfixed, at the little rivers of blood creeping from the body.

"Magee!" Seeler shouted. Grasping the little man by the collar he propelled him forcefully out of the front door and along the path. He did not look around, but was conscious of faces peering through parted curtains. Then they were back in the van, swaying as Norm took a corner at an alarming tilt.

"All done?" Dessi asked from the front seat. Seeler said nothing, but for Magee the question was a cue to begin babbling. "Brilliantly! Dominic was so cool..." he went on to describe in explicit detail the events up to the shooting, embroidering and glorifying in the manner of those who dream of action but never partake.

"Bang bang." He emptied the whole magazine into the bastard. Left him bleeding all over the carpet. Good one. Good one." And he looked at Seeler with something like pride in his eyes.

Later, when they were safely ensconced in the lodgings, Dessi sought out the big man and found him staring into the open fire in a contemplative mood. He joined him at the fireside.

"You've done this before. That much was plain from the way you went about the job. From the way you finished him off to the way you made your exit. You're good, and it's a

pleasure to be working with you, but you don't like it do you?"
Seeler looked at him with those eyes of deep grey, and replied: "To be truthful, Dessi, I gave up worrying about killing years ago, but it still has an effect on me. I just like to sit quiet for a while, y'know?"

Dessi nodded. "Gotcha." Placing a hand on Seeler's shoulder, he got to his feet. "You'll be seeing less of the outsiders from now on; the Magees of this world. I could see how much he was annoying you. Mebbe see you later for a drink, eh?"

After midnight Seeler walked the streets. He was in, he knew that. He had passed with flying colours. Yet the achievement gave him little satisfaction. To banish his unease he set about plotting a way to place Dessi into the hands of the authorities. He was making his way to a meeting with his SAS contact when he was alerted by a tingling in his stomach. Years of living on a knife edge had developed him a cast iron gut, but a sensitive one. He had learned long ago to trust his instincts, and he knew he was being followed!

Melting into the gloom of a doorway, pressing himself in until his shape was invisible in the blackness, he waited. His breathing was slow and measured, his hands placed for motion.

Jimmy appeared. He moved well, few people would have spotted him. If his own well-developed sixth sense had not warned him he might have led the Irishman right to the SAS contact and given away the whole package. Jimmy passed, and Seeler, moving with the weight and fluidity of a shadow, trod in his wake. With a rapid movement he snaked one arm around Jimmy's neck, with his other fitting an immobilising and painful wristlock. "Dominic?" Jimmy's voice shook.

"Why the chaperon service, Jimmy boy?" Seeler muttered into his ear. His tone was menacing. When Jimmy was slow responding he gave the wrist a sharp twist that forced a squeal from him.

"Okay okay," Jimmy wheezed; the big man's forearm across his throat made breathing difficult. "We have to be careful. You're still new. You don't know your way around. We can't afford you getting into trouble."

"Fourteen years, Jimmy. Fourteen years in strange lands, living with death everyday. You think I can't smell a tail a mile off?"

Jimmy conceded the point, adding, in a frightened voice: "I was acting on orders, Dominic. You know, orders. I know you're alright. Honest."

Before releasing him, Seeler searched his coat and unearthed an ancient-looking Webley. Tipping the bullets into his hand he pocketted them and returned the weapon to Jimmy's waistband. "If you're carrying when you tail me again, Jimmy, I'll take it personally, and kill you. Understand?"

He let go. Jimmy took to his heels and vanished into the night.

Seeler turned back towards the house. For the first time since the mission had begun, he felt the glow of satisfaction in his gut.

*

11:

Jack Burt met Stanley Murdoch in a small country pub renowned for it's real ales. Horse brasses adorned the black beamed walls, and the locals sat in cliques around old tables, eyeing the strangers with faintly hostile indifference.

Jack ferried two brimming pints to the table. Murdoch took a long draught and smacked his lips. "That's good. That's very, very good."

Jack tried his pint, decided he did not like it, and embarked upon the conversation. "Well, Mr Murdoch, it's been eleven days. Do you have anything for me?"

Murdoch nodded his head. "It was slow starting, but I think I've made up most of the ground. What I can tell you is that the police were not at fault; it's plain they weren't allowed to make too much progress." Jack frowned, baffled, but Murdoch asked for patience. Hoisting his briefcase onto the table, he took out a tatty file. "First though...I think you ought to read this."

Jack took the file and flipped it open. "Newspaper clippings." He read through some of them, then glanced up, a puzzled frown creasing his brow. "Terrorists die in a shoot out with French police? So what?"

"That's the published version. It's not the whole story. A friend of mine, in Special Branch, came up with the goods."

As he listened, Jack doodled on the clippings with a pen. Murdoch commented: "An Irish group, thought to be a splinter of the IRA have been buying arms and smuggling them across Europe. They are one of the smaller groups in Northern Ireland. Until recently they were a largely ignored group. They began as a protest organisation, but a combination of circumstances, making no headway with political initatives, and being crushed almost out of existance by the the Provos and the other hardliners, led the group, the Ulster Liberation Council, to become hardline themselves. But they have taken to the offensive with ferocity, recently launching a series of attacks on RUC offices, and even a string of firebombings here on the mainland...."

"If I'm honest, Mr Murdoch, I can't say I know too much about the situation over there..."

Murdoch nodded. "It is complicated. Suffice to say it's a cauldron, a guerrilla war made up of tit-for-tat strikes. The British Army and the police forced to operate as though in a war in some foreign land. The Republicans, the IRA for example, get a lot of funding from America - where of course a sizeable block of the population is of Irish descent. And there is aid from other quarters; guns and ammunition, as well as money, from places like Libya, where dictatorships see the Irish struggle as a stick they can use to beat the 'western oppressers' with."

Jack reined in his impatience. "I'd like to know where this is leading."

"The ties between the ULC and the IRA are complicated and confused. Suffice to say the Active Service Unit was hit not by the French police, but by a couple of British Intelligence agents from a Counter-Terrorist unit known as Covert Resources, or CORE. The aim was to cut off the flow of weapons. The British have enough to deal with, keeping the IRA at bay. The policy is; the ULC are to be made ineffective, or eliminated. There was a woman among the dead. See her there?" Jack referred to the text. "Mary Morrison?" Murdoch nodded. He said:"She was a bomb maker. A fanatical hater of the British. She lived with a man named Culum Strong. He's a middle level IRA cell commander. A very dangerous man indeed. Obviously he was distressed, and he swore revenge."

With the pen, Jack impatiently drew a circle around the dead woman's name. "Where is this leading?"

"The story about the French police is a cover. CORE does not exist, officially. The man who killed Mary Morrison is called Colin Congreave. Does that name ring a bell?"

Burt shook his head. "Should it?" Murdoch remained silent, but kept on staring at him. Jack racked his brain, then was almost felled by realisation. "We bought the house from a couple named Congreave. My God, do you think there's a connection?"

"I'm afraid so. One and the same man. The revenge strike came a few days too late. They must have ..."

"They thought Carol was his wife, and the kids...." The pen fell from his fingers. He covered his face."Mary. Written all over the walls...in blood." He started to cry.

Murdoch sipped disconsolately at his beer until Jack was able to compose himself. A few of the pub regulars directed curious glances at them, but kept their distance.

At last, and with a mighty sigh, Jack emerged from behind his hands. "Where's Congreave now? Does he know?

Murdoch nodded. "I believe so. I managed to learn his new address. He has not been seen for over two weeks. From my friend in Special Branch I gather he's a specialist in Counter-terrorism. He's paid to remove them. He must have guessed the reason for the murders and put his family in safekeeping. Now you know what I know."

Jack leaned his head on his hands while he thought. Murdoch, having finished his pint, shuffled uncomfortably on his seat for a while before deciding to get up to buy another. When he returned with a brimming glass it was to find Burt sitting with a steely resolve on his face. He sat down.

"Okay, Mr Murdoch..." Jack began in a low voice. "Here's what we are going to do. Firstly, I want to meet Congreave. I have to meet him..." he waved down the beginnings of Murdoch's protest. "You are going to reach whoever is in charge of this special unit in British Intelligence and make it clear that unless I receive the co-operation I need, this story is going to appear in newspapers worldwide. They won't shut me up."

Murdoch was shaking his head. "Mr Burt..."

"Secondly, you are going to help get me into shape. Find me a place in some military establishment if you can. I was in Vietnam, I can handle myself, I just need a little sharpening up. Lastly, I want you to get me a weapon. I'm going to find this Culum Strong, and I'm going to kill him."

Murdoch swallowed. "Please, Mr Burt, forget all this. If you don't get yourself killed you'll get yourself arrested. Put the past behind you. You can't possibly win."

Jack's eyes blazed coldly. "I am going to put the past behind me, just as soon as I've finished what I set out to do. I'll be going ahead, with or without you, but as I'm paying why not stay in for the ride?"

Murdoch looked doubtful. At length he sighed. "Yes Sir, you're paying. I'll help you as far as getting a weapon and finding Culum Strong, but then our agreement terminates and I want paying in full. That's my only condition."

"Accepted." snapped Jack. The intense expression remained on his face a few moments longer, then the mood broke and he smiled. "Another pint? It's my shout."

12:

The cold night wind whistled hollowly throughout the unfinished houses on the site. Meeting at midnight, Seeler mused cynically to himself. How melodramatic.

The low murmuring of a man humming a melody guided him to the rendezvous spot where his SAS contact crouched in a black corner, patiently smoking a cigarette. The two exchanged greetings, and Seeler reported his part in the McGowan killing. There was silence after the telling, then the SAS officer extinguished his cigarette and let out a sigh. "We wondered about that. The description the RUC got from McGowan's wife fitted you perfectly."

Sensing disapproval, Seeler spoke out. "Don't judge me, Colonel. It was either kill him or blow the infiltration. As things stand, I'll be in deep enough to reach my targets before too long."

"I understand that, Seeler, and for my part I think you did the right thing. But we're a different breed. Try sell it to the folks back home."

A familiar rush of frustration set Seeler's blood fizzing; he hated the dual role of point man and scapegoat, but settling himself, he explained his ideas for the capture of Dessi O'Bain. The plan was listened to, considered, then agreed to.

"Ideally we ought to have official sanction for this, but if we take the time we need to set that up too many people will have to know and we'll increase the risk; we already know even our best units leak. No, we'll do it your way. Limit the potential damage."

In the darkness Seeler smiled. He was grateful, he knew the risk from officialdom the Colonel was running, given him rein like this. "Once I'm on the run, let the police put everything they have into the search. Nothing less will convince the IRA leaders that I'm kosher. And nothing less will force them to come to my aid."

The Colonel fitted the tiny transmitter behind the wide collar on Seeler's thick jacket, checked that it was secure, then flattened the collar and took a backward step. "There, we can keep tabs on you from a safe distance."

"Make sure you do. Dessi's been dropping hints. we could be moving at any time."

The Colonel nodded. "I'll supervise this operation personally. We want friend Dessi pretty badly. We'll be on the ball."

Soon afterwards they parted for the final time. The Colonel climbed into a vehicle that passed on a regular sweep, while Seeler picked his way across the broken paths that networked the site.

*

Seeler was woken rudely by Dessi in the middle of the night. He woke to a feeling of intense fear - for the first time in years he had been caught unawares while sleeping; usually his inner alarms functioned perfectly. Could he really have been that tired, he wondered, or was he losing his edge?

Determining to be better prepared in future, he struggled upright in the sleeping bag and asked Dessi what was happening. The killer's voice was lowered to a sibilant hiss, hard-edged and frightening. "Time to be going, Dominic. We've a man to meet. Come on."

Shrugging on his thick jacket, Seeler followed Dessi into the sparse kitchen. A blackened kettle, bubbling noisily on the ancient and smelly cooker, began to whistle. Dessi poured boiling water into two mugs primed with instant coffee and sugar, and in silence the two men downed the heartening liquid. Seeler was careful not to appear too inquisitive; O'Bain would only have his suspicious aroused. Besides, he reminded himself, if SAS Colonel Phillips was as good as his word, Dessi would never reach his destination.

A battered Bedford van stood in the dank garage adjacent to the house. The van doors slid open on hanging runners, and the interior was riddled with draughtholes, but the engine, when Dessi roused it, growled like a thoroughbred.

"They've done a great job on this. She goes like a dream."

Seeler opened the garage doors, and closed them again once the Irishman had driven out the van. Then he leapt into the passenger seat and they turned on a southerly route out of the city. Rain teemed, and the windows were blurred despite the steady industry of the wipers. Dessi stared ahead. His face looked hollow in the thin light, eyes rheumy through lack of solid sleep. Casually, Seeler leaned against the door and cupped his left hand under his cheek, as though trying to nap. Glancing at him, Dessi gave a wry smile; Dominic was a cool one alright!

Seeler's thumb located the transmitter beneath his collar. Sought and found the tiny slide control on the device and engaged it. Monitoring the signal on sensitive equipment housed in an armoured van, the SAS officer-of-the-watch noted the change in tone from the transmitter, the rapid beeping. He addressed the soldier at the console: "This is it. As soon as you have a reading, plot the route out of town. We have sites primed. As soon as they hit a deserted stretch of road, we move in." Lifting the radio telephone receiver from the console, he called Colonel Philips at his billet.

"He's on the move, Sir."

Shifting from his bed, the Colonel replaced the receiver and suppressed a yawn. He was finding instant readiness a strain, and knew he had been on this tour too long. Trust O'Bain to move in the dead of night. With an effort of will he forced himself upright and briskly began to dress.

The streetlamps ended abruptly as they left the town limits. The sudden descent of near total blackness came as a small shock. The feeble probing of the headlamps, the elongated halo of the beams as they converged, illuminated fleetingly the road that rushed underneath them, and the narrow corridor of looming foliage that hurtled past the windows. Dessi gripped the wheel grimly. His eyes ached from the effort of peering ahead. A glance spared for his companion revealed that the big man was sleeping peacefully. Once more he envied Dominic's composure under pressure. Ahead, the intense sweeping blackness was interrupted by a cluster of lights. Vehicles, but not moving. Dessi frowned and immediately feared the worst. The beams from the vehicles clashed, telling him they were parked at angles. "Roadblock," he muttered. "Jaysus." Roughly he shook Seeler awake. "Dominic, trouble ahead."

Seeler had been expecting the move.Feigning dullness, as though emerging from sleep, he smothered a yawn, then jerked upright in his seat. "Garda, d'you think?"

"Or worse," growled Dessi."If they look at all unfriendly I'll put my foot down. They'll have to chase us."

"No," Seeler disagreed. "Better to go on foot. It's pitch black out there, we can break across the fields. Unless they have dogs they won't be able to pin us down."

The lights were nearer, brighter, dark shapes could be discerned, breaking the beams as they moved. "Uniforms." Dessi breathed. "Oh feck."

"No way through." Seeler joined in. Dessi was now breathing hard, preparing himself for the clash. "We're not far from Murphy's farm; it's a safe place. Four miles west of here. You go for it as soon as I brake. I'll meet you there. You ready?"

Seeler was. The van slewed wildly as Dessi pressed down the brake. The shadows began to run towards them. They carried weapons.

Seeler hit the earth at a roll, and, with barely a pause to orient himself, plunged through the thick hedge by the roadside and landed flatfooted in the field beyond. He began to run. His heavy boots sank into the sucking, spongy earth but he hammered on, drawing deep regular breaths, mustering his strength.

The SAS Colonel cocked his weapon as he sprinted towards the driver's side of the van. He knew O'Bain would be driving. He had waited a long time to take him and he was determined not to waste the opportunity. He saw the Irishman leap from the van and glance quickly about him, then prepare to spring for the black shroud of night.

"Freeze Dessi!" He yelled, aiming from the hip. The Irishman hesitated the briefest instant, then sprang. All hell broke loose. The Colonel fired, other shadows joining in, some firing at Dessi, others at the elusive second man who had dived for the hedge. Bullets ripped at Dessi, spinning him around as he fell, with a cry, to the soft earth.

"CEASE FIRE!" Yelled the Colonel. The sudden silence rang on the damp air.

Seeler ran on. His lungs burned, but as long as the bullets kicked up earth at his heels, he ran on. When the order rang out, and the firing stopped, he heaved a sigh and eased the pace a little. Spotting a dark mass on the horizon, trees, he changed tack, plunging on, intent only on securing a safe place for the night. He could not afford to be taken. Not if he was to succeed in reaching the other members, the inner circle, of the ULC. Arriving at the trees he ploughed on heedlessly. Rough branches gouged his cheeks and tore at his hands. The sounds of his passing: the crashing through the trees, the thudding of his boots, the heavy rhythmic breathing, emphasised the totality of the silence and not the other way around. A safe place, his mind repeatedly. A safe place!

The Colonel placed his fingertips alongside Dessi's neck. A pulse throbbed faintly. "He's still alive," he shouted. "Get a stretcher!"

While Dessi was carefully placed on a stretcher and carried into a vehicle for transportation to the nearest hospital, the Colonel stood beside the Bedford and watched the party of pursuers returning, bedraggled, through the gap in the hedge created by Seeler as he leapt from the van.

"It's no good, Sir." The leader of the unit reported. "It's impossible to spot him. It's too dark, and the ground too muddy. We need dogs."

Colonel Philips nodded, bade the men prepare to leave. Alone for a moment he stared into the gloom.

"It's up to you now, old friend," he whispered. "Good Luck."

13:

News of Dessi's capture hogged the headlines the following day. He was the biggest catch the authorities had landed for a while, and his association with firebombings, and the controversial death of a British soldier, made them determined to make the most of the situation. He lay in hospital with fifteen wounds in him. One bullet had passed within an inch of a vital artery. He was not expected to live.

IRA Chieftains were alarmed by the seizure, for it meant they had to suspect a high level leak in their organisation. A dreaded stinking tout in their midst. They were dismayed too by the news that their latest recruit, the indomitable Dominic, was on the run. The word went out; favours were called in, contacts set to work. The big man was to be found, sheltered, and delivered safely.

On the mainland Dessi's demise was greeted with joy by the armed and security services. The man had gotten what was coming to him. Government spokesmen praised the work of the army and talked of the effective liason between the RUC and the military. Because Seeler's true role was a secret the word went out; find Dominic, and destroy him!

Jack Burt had been summoned to meet Stanley Murdoch at the same pub. Murdoch had hinted on the telephone that he had important information, and Jack sat impatiently tasting a triple Canadian Club with dry ginger.When Murdoch came in, his brisk, but slightly bowed large frame wrapped in a volumous overcoat, Jack got to his feet and ordered a pint. By the time he carried it to the table Murdoch was ready to talk. Taking a sip from his glass, he sighed, then hoisted his briefcase onto his lap. He drew out a sheaf of papers, tapped them on the tabletop, then drew a breath.

"I think we have a break through." he sounded almost smug. A great deal of his time on the job was spent on stupid and boring surveillance work, following errant spouses, logging the to-ing and fro-ing of shady characters, and digging up lost relatives. With this case, he had found, or rather re-discovered, the joys of his job. A chance to use his initiative, to use his contacts, to flex his muscles. He was feeling important. He relished the prospect of exhibiting his expertise to Jack Burt.

"First, our boy Culum is not working alone. He has a lifelong friend, a man called Finnabr Craig with him on his revenge mission. They're the ones who committed the assault on your family."

Jack interrupted. "Are you sure? The police seemed positive the killer was alone. There was no forensic evidence to indicate a second man."

"I don't know about that. Maybe what you were told was intended to tie in with the cover story; the motiveless murder. No one could have foreseen you taking matters into your own hands. You've got the screw turning, and doors are starting to open. What I have learned is that Culum never works alone, and this is where we start to run into the inconsistencies."

"Oh?" Jack's interest was piqued. There was an infuriating pause while Murdoch drank.

"Yes, the things that don't ring true. Firstly, an IRA revenge strike on the mainland just doesn't happen. When they send an ASU over here it is the result of meticulous planning. They don't have the resources to squander manpower and weapons on actions that fall outside their normal theatre of operations. They place bombs in public places, they commit sectarian killings, they murder high ranking public officials. What they don't do is send someone over here on a personal vendetta. So conclusion number one is that the strike on your family, even though it was intended to hurt Congreave, was unlikely to be an official IRA action. Culum and Finnbar were hunting on their own time."

"Do you know any more about them? Do we have any photgraphs?"

"No pictures. Never arrested, never even questioned or fingerprinted.These boys didn't even show up for the school photographer, and once they went in deep cover for the Provos, all of the photographs held by their families were taken. You see, because they weren't in the system, they were invisible men, and their value to the Provos was incalculable."

"So, what DO we know?"

"We know that Finnbar is tolerated because of his link to Culum. Culum could go far in the IRA. He's intelligent. He can plan, and he weighs the risks. Finnbar's a virtual psychopath. Uncontrollable. He'll take what he wants when he wants, be it food, money, another man's woman. He causes trouble. He's hated, and he's feared. Not an organisation man. He'll never be more than a hired gun to the Provos."

"What we'd call a loose cannon." Jack mused.

"Exactly. A nutter."

"So at least we know we're not going up against an entire terrorist organisation. It's them and me." He glanced up towards the bar. A tv set on a wall bracket caught his attention. The sound was low, but audible. The news; headline, the capture of Dessi O'Bain. "I bet this guy, Dessi, could lead us to Culum Strong. Do you think we could get in to see him?"

Murdoch shook his head in near despair. "Absolutely not. You have to understand something, Mr Burt. To get what I've got now I had to tread on some pretty big toes.Only sympathy with the position you're in got us through."

"But as we're leaning on the Home Office anyway, why not lean a little harder?"

Murdoch cautioned against this, saying: "Believe me, they'll only put up with so much threatening. If you become too much of a nuisance they'll feel impelled to act, and that could get serious."

Jack looked at him, then he laughed weakly. "You're not suggesting anything could happen to me, are you...?" In response, Murdoch moved an eyebrow. Jack felt shaken. "Come on, this is Great Britain, not some dictatorship." Murdoch remained silent. Jack lapsed into silence.

Murdoch ordered refilled glasses, and turned the conversation to the toughening up course he had laid on for his client. "The place is perfect. Cold, isolated, the ideal location to get away from it all and concentrate on sharpening up. The courses are hard, and come highly recommended, but they are not cheap. Two weeks will leave you no change out of a thousand pounds."

Jack nodded "Good." His eyes glittered with cold relish at the thought of actually DOING something. "I can hardly wait. Any news on the weapon?"

On this, Murdoch was less committal. "It's a tall order and I have to tread carefully. If I go stomping in I'll scare off the supplier," he lied. Privately he had decided that supplying his client with a gun was not worth the risk. "By the time you get back from PRISM, I hope to have more news for you."

Jack looked puzzled. "Prism, what's that?" Murdoch replied: "The camp you're going to." He smiled. "I've heard it's hell on earth."

14:

"PRISM, gentlemen. What is it?" David Parsons paced before the blackboard as he delivered his customary address to the latest intake. "PRISM is an acronym derived from the title of the course we run here: Protective Response Instruction and Survival Management. And that, in a nutshell, sums up the course exactly. If we do our jobs right you will become physically and mentally fitter than you've been for years. You will learn how to handle dangerous situations, how to survive in the wild. I can promise you a number of things. You will suffer, you will become disenchanted, you will grow to hate us. But ultimately you will triumph, conquer your weaknesses and emerge stronger than ever with a fresher view of life. You will have discovered and tapped into the great inner resources dormant within you. You will come to love us, and, finally..." he smiled, "You will be glad you came."

"I shall hand you over now to my good friend Sam Ellis who will walk you through the induction. Explain the routines and what is expected of each of you." he inserted a pause for effect. "Gain through pain, gentlemen. Say goodbye to your old selves. You will never be the same men again."

As Parsons left the room, one man applauded limply, and was quickly silenced by the uncomfortable quiet that enveloped the gathering. Then Sam Ellis, thin and wiry, square of jaw, and pale skinned, with eyes that looked too large for his gaunt face, and with tatty, cropped red hair, stepped energetically up on to the dais and scanned the audience with a look of steely contempt.

"First things first. Here you are nobody. Your money

buys you nothing, your position buys you no sympathy, no priviledges. You are nothing, and nothing you think or say means a damm thing to me. So let's start as we mean to continue. SIT UP STRAIGHT!"

His fog-horn voice sent a jolt through the assembled men. It was a huge voice, blasting resoundingly from copper-lined lungs. At the back of the room, a half smile moved on Jack Burt's face. Just like boot camp!

*

15:

With the dawn came rain, hurtling down in great slanting sheets between massed trees. The ground becoming steadily boggier as he ran. Breath came in rasping snatches, and in desperation he was forced to plunge deep within himself to find the strength to go on. Then he was out of the trees and careering down a steep grassy slope, greasy with rain and slick underfoot, his arms flailing as he fought for balance. His face muscles were taut as he focused on not stumbling. He hit the level and immediately sank knee deep in thick mire. He ploughed on, desperation increasing as the yelping of the dogs on his trail grew louder, and the faint shouts of the handlers were carried on the still morning air. He forced himself onward, determined to beat the clinging mud, though all he really wanted to do was find a hole and rest.

His progress seemed to halt. The mud sucked him in, and though he gritted his teeth, and grunted, and struggled with all his might, and whimpered in frustration, he could not improve on the maddening crawl. The sounds of pursuit grew nearer. His breathing was fast and hollow, each breath forcing a small cry from him. Then just as suddenly the mire solidified beneath his feet and he was climbing free of it, his boots skidding, but gripping, on the sloping bank. He was running, wildly, not in any particular direction, simply filled with elation at the sudden prospect of escape.

A pond loomed and he was unable to swerve in time. He sprawled headlong into the still, icy black water, and when he raised his head, sputtering, it was to find himself incapable of movement. His muscles had locked solid. He could not raise himself. The water's chill had clutched his breath and refreshed his wits, but he lay there, suspended on his arms, too tired even to moan in frustration.

The hounds closed in hungrily; yelps sounding like horns blown in triumph. And he thought; 'Why fight it?'

A ring of men surrounded him. Grimfaced, holding fierce dogs on taut leashes, shotguns crooked over arms. He glanced around at them, accepting the inevitable. But they said nothing, merely studied him with blank indifference. His face, lined with fatigue and coursed with the black residue of the pond, looked askance at them, wary.

With an almighty effort he hauled himself to his feet. His clothes were saturated and heavy, and the sound of the water pouring from him as he stood was the only disturbance in that tranquil dawn air save the panting of the dogs. "Okay," he panted, mustering a wry grimace. "It's a fair cop."

A dog growled, others joined in, then one of the handlers snatched his shotgun into position, the weapon setting with a frightening snap. One by one the others followed suit until Seeler found himself surrounded by the blank, double-barrelled stares.

"Hey," he gasped, slowly raising his hands. "I give up."

Then he was screaming as the triggers were pulled and the dawn was shattered by the multiple blasts. He was hurled backwards by the force of being struck, he was falling...

He jerked upright in the bed of rough planking. Sweat was pouring from him, and his chest rose and fell at an alarming rate. His ears still rang with echoes of the gunshots.

It was a dream, he kept telling himself. Just a dream. Daylight flooded in through the tiny square of glass set high up the wall. The light was soft, greenish, and reminded him that he was in a cellar, the window framed by thick grass. Murphy's farm.

On clambering from the bed he reeled dizzily and had to clutch at a chair back to steady himself. A cracked basin clung limply to one wall. He lunged for it, turned the rusty faucet and splashed brownish, icy water onto his face. He felt himself straightening. Looking into the speckled mirror hung from a nail above the basin, he was disturbed by the haggardness of the visage peering back at him. This was a high pressure assignment, but had the fear really gotten to him that much? Calling upon the vast inner resources he had stockpiled over years of living on a knife edge, he controlled the fear and pushed himself away from the basin. When he turned back to the bed his shoulders had squared and his mouth tightened. With measured movements he quickly dressed and went upstairs to the farmhouse kitchen.

Eddie O'Hare had bought Murphy's farm a decade before, and anyone seeing the way he ran the place would wonder how he stayed in business. But he was useful to the Provos, and a meaningful portion of the funds channelled each year to the organisation was devoted to keeping Murphy's farm a going concern.

O'Hare was an early riser. He had milked the few cows the farm supported, and was in the kitchen when Seeler wandered in. The smell of bacon frying made the big man's mouth water.

O'Hare smiled over his shoulder. "G'morning, Dominic." He was a perpetually cheerful man. The knowledge that his homestead was safe, buttressed as it was by NORAID funds, had gotten him into the habit of not worrying about life. He whistled as he transferred the bacon from pan to plate. Seeler sat down and helped himself to bread and butter.

"Tea's fresh." declared Eddie, placing the plate before the big man. He took the seat opposite and poured himself a cup. He said: "The Garda passed by again in the night. Our contact in the ranks may not be able to stall them much longer." He quickly explained that a senior police official had been reached. Under threat to his family he had falsified a report indicating that the farm had been thoroughly searched and nothing found. Even so, the possibility that another patrol would stop at the farm was worrying.

"Better be ready to move today." O'Hare warned. "Five days is the longest anyone has ever stayed here. I expect you'll be shipped by nightfall."

Munching, Seeler nodded. O'Hare looked slightly uncomfortable for a moment, then said: "There was news of Dessi this morning. On the radio." Seeler looked up. "He's going to live. The bastards have him under massive guard in hospital. As soon as he's well enough they'll have him on trial. They'll throw the book at him." Sadly he shook his head. "Imagine surviving fifteen bullet wounds to face that. He'd be better off dead."

Seeler displayed commiseration. He looked calm, but was racking his brains trying to formulate a plan that would allow him to contact the SAS Colonel. A raid at the right moment, if he could arrange it, would give the authorities the chance to clean up. But the telephone was in a locked room, and he was forbidden to leave the house. He had tried to slip out the first night, but three vicious looking alsation dogs started howling and he was forced to retreat in stealth to his cellar.

As O'Hare busied himself with the washing up, Seeler sat back on his chair, satiated, and willed himself to be patient.

The first three days had been the worst. Now, although Jack Burt's muscles still ached, the ache was good, not crucifying, and his breathing and general well-being had improved immeasurably. There had even been moments when his grief had receded, when he had actually forgotten. And though he experienced some guilt over this occurring, he accepted it as a healing sign.

He had been up at dawn with the others, and had led the pack every yard of a five mile run. A quick hot shower had been followed by a hearty breakfast. Late morning found his group in the gym, practising breakfalls on thin mats. Although some of the men felt foolish, falling to the floor, and some felt bruised, none dared object and even the weakest members were embraced by the growing sense of camaraderie in the group.

They were learning to fall sideways, take the fall on a shoulder, roll until almost upright, then fall back again along the same arc, shoulders functioning pretty much like the rockers on a child's toy rocking horse. Left, right, falling, rising, the surroundings lost in a blur. Never quite righting oneself. Back and forth along the arc until the stomach gave. One by one the group members fell aside. Some reeling, others vomiting into buckets provided. But good old Jack Burt rolled on. Good ole rockin' Jack. Determined to prove himself, determined to make it. Stomach clamped tight, concentration fierce. Intent only on being the last to quit. He rolled until the instructor called a halt, then he stood upright, vision swimming, body swaying, holding on, aware of the looks from the others; envy, spite, open admiration.

The afternoon session was devoted to close-quarter combat drill. Instilling the killer-edge, the strike-first initiative. Jack, having been in the army and having served in Vietnam, knew the rudiments - in him they simply lay dormant. When the tough instructor took him aside for a little more intense tuition most of the old skills he'd known re-emerged, if a little rustily.

The instructor suddenly told him to rest. Jack was glad to; he was panting, sweat poured from his brow. He squatted, back pressed to the cool wall, and felt the dampness of his karate *gi*. He felt good despite the aching in his muscles and the violent sinuation of his chest as his lungs filled and emptied.

He glanced toward the door where the instructor was talking with two men who had just entered the gym. One of the men he recognised; Parsons, the owner of the camp. Jack had met him and felt touched by his calm. The second man was thin, but appeared fit and strong. He had fair hair, cut neat, and a narrow face that carried a slightly haunted expression. His large hands flexed involuntarily at his sides. His stance was not relaxed. There was an edginess to him, a tension. He stood as if ready to repel attack. A total, complete contrast to the serene Parsons. Jack saw the men dart glances in his direction and he began to feel uneasy. Then Parsons broke away and approached him with that deceptive, easy smile on his face. But as Parsons drew nearer Jack saw that the smile was strained and false. And when he looked into Parsons' eyes he saw that something had disturbed the calm. He felt a wave of unease break over him; whatever it was, Parsons was not anxious to talk about it.

Conscious that all eyes were on them, the two men stared at each other. "Jack, would you come up to my office please? We have something important to discuss."

Movement attracted Jack's gaze. He saw the other man, the stranger, leave the gym. An inexplicable sense of urgency gripped him, he rose stiffly. When they reached the office, Parsons stood aside to let Jack enter first. The stranger was there, and next to him sat Stanley Murdoch. Parsons shut the door and took the seat behind the desk.

The silence was awkward. Puzzlement shone on Jack's face. He looked to Murdoch. "Stan, what's going on?"

The private detective stood out of his seat. He looked grossly uncomfortable. So too did Parsons. There was an electricity in the air. "Mr Burt," Murdoch began, shaking hands. "You're looking good, Sir." He glanced at the stranger, as though unsure how to continue, then he cleared his throat. He indicated the stranger. "Let me introduce you to Colin Congreave."

The news struck him like a dash of icy water. There were no handshakes, he was capable of nothing more than a muttered acknowledgement. Then the four took adversarial positions around the desk. Drinks were poured, and Jack listened in amazement to Murdoch's explanation.

"My pressuring the Home Office on your behalf had some effect. I got through to Sir Alastair Watson. He's some bigwig in intelligence. He knew that he could put you and Mr Congreave in touch, and thought here might be a suitable place to meet. He decided to come down on the side of the angels. He wants Culum Strong and Co out of business as much as you do."

Jack swivelled his gaze to fix upon the man he had conditioned himself to hate. During the training, the lonely hours, the painful runs, his mind had focused on a single idea; facing Congreave. He had clung ferociously to this idea. Now he half expected the man to yield under the unremitting glare. But Congreave did not. Then Jack recalled the description Murdoch had supplied that day in the pub. Congreave was paid to eliminate terrorists. He was a killer. He would not quail. In a voice brittle with tension, Congreave spoke: "I just want you to know I'm as committed as you are to the destruction of those men."

Jack felt a sneer burn his face. It felt branded there. "Oh yeah? Enough to wish you were in my shoes, your family butchered and buried?"

Parsons voice softly divided the chasm between them. "Sarcasm is so ugly, Jack. And so revealing."

But Jack continued to glower. Congreave had averted his head, and Jack felt a certain sick satisfaction; he had struck a nerve.

"No," Colin murmured. "I can't say I wish that. My family is every bit as precious to me as ---"

"AS MINE WAS?!!" Jack screamed. He was out of his seat, fingers half clenched and stiff, like claws. "At least in your case there would be a reason!"

"Sit down Jack." Parsons commanded calmly. Jack looked at him, poured anger at him, but Parsons simply returned the stare with that intractable calm of his, and Jack felt his anger bleed away. He sat down.

Murdoch cleared his throat. He toyed with his glass, tilting it this way and that. "Mr Congreave wants to put right as much as he can. He is willing to place his considerable skills at your disposal in order to find and eliminate the men who killed your family."

Jack's breathing was hard and nasal. "That's very big of him."

"I can't put things right!" Congreave blasted right back at him. "Much as I'd like to, I can't do it. But you want justice, revenge, and I'm going to help you get it."

Jack felt stranded, momentarily had no words. He struggled to begin a protest, but Parsons overrode him.

"For now, Jack, why not accept Colin's offer? I've

known him for years. I believe him. And if you really are determined to go ahead I can think of no better man to have at your side."

Jack smouldered silently. He could accept Congreave's word - part of him knew that. Through the mist of anger he could dimly see and sympathise with Congreave's own anxieties - the need to pre-empt an attack on his family. But he could not forgive the fates for placing his wife and children in the path of Culum Strong's vengeance. He could not forgive.

"Alright," he breathed."We can work together. But that doesn't mean we have to socialise." Thrusting himself upright he stalked from the room.

*

16:

As dusk fired the sky, burnishing the strata of low cloud to a searing gold, a British Army Saracen vehicle trundled into the yard outside Murphy's farmhouse and braked noisily. Sitting in the kitchen with O'Hare, Seeler saw the vehicle through the window and leapt to his feet in fright. "Christ!"

O'Hare unleashed a wider than usual smile. "Relax, Dom boy, it's one of ours."

A plainly dressed man clambered from the vehicle. Seeing Seeler through the window, he waved. The big man gave a half hearted wave in return.

"Better get your kit." O'Hare grinned.

The driver was Norm Nunny. He greeted Dominic warmly and they set off, following the road to the west. The cab was warm, the engine a comforting rumble, and they had travelled a mile or so before Norm spoke again. "So, how've you been?"

"No complaints. Shame about Dessi." Norm muttered his agreement. "Bastards." he said. "You were lucky."

"I was."

Norm could no longer cork the subject he had been holding down. "We'll be taking you to meet Culum Strong tonight.You heard of him?"

Seeler appeared to think for a moment. Then with a downward turn of his mouth, he shook his head. "Should I have?"

"No reason you should, I suppose. What with you being away so long. He replaced old McFee when the Pigs took him."

Seeler chuckled. "Him I remember. He put me right a few times. It was he wanted me full time in the cause."

Norm joined him in a smile. "Aye."

Seeler dared a question. "We going far?"

Norm's mouth pursed as his smile slid into a sly grin. "Not as far as you might think."

The Saracen ground to a halt inside a stonewalled garage attached to a rambling country house set in considerable grounds. Norm cut the engine and, unseen in the darkness, someone pulled shut the garage door. Lights flickered on as Seeler stepped out, and a stocky man with a rounded, rather boyish, but humourless face, with eyes of cold brown and black curly hair, stepped forward with outstretched hand.

"Culum Strong, Dominic. Pleased to meet you." His voice, though abrupt, had a gentle lilt.

"And you...Culum." Seeler affected shyness. Dominic was known to be bashful when in the limelight.

Snaking an arm around the big man's vast shoulders, Culum led him through to the house. "Come on, my friend, we'll drink to celebrate your homecoming."

*

Outside the gymnasium windows, night curtained off the magnificent wild mountain vista with a velvet screen. The windows rattled gently in their frames as the night wind came whistling down the valley basin. Jack Burt was alone in the gym, restlessly drifting from one piece of apparatus to another. A thick-bodied bag hung invitingly, and he could not resist a swipe at it. There was a satisfying thud as his fist struck and the bag swung along an uneven parabola. Settling into a wider stance he began to rain blows on the canvass. The bag reacted unpredictably to the asault and his breath came in loud gasps as he struggled to pin it down, to master it. At last he halted, let the bag slap against his chest. He rested his cheek against the cool, coarse fabric and felt grief envelope him with renewed vigour. It filled his chest, the grief, seemed to want to wrest out his heart. Meeting Congreave had done him no good at all.

He stood that way for long minutes. Aching. Barely able to suppress tears. Longing to find a small dark room where he could just let go....

The door swung open on whining hinges and Colin Congreave entered. The door flapped shut behind him, and for long moments the two men stared at each other.

"I'm sorry about your family, Jack." Colin crossed the room, halting a few feet short.

"Save the goo. We're not on first name terms, Congreave, and we're never going to be friends."

"But we are going to have to work together." Colin persisted. "Have to rely on each other. Learn to trust --"

"NO NO NO!" Jack thundered, pushing away the bag. He rounded on Congreave. "Don't preach to me about trust and reliance. I had children who relied on me, trusted me, to keep them safe! Your actions put paid to that."

"I know it. Don't you think I know that? Don't you think I'm hurting?"

"I don't care what you are feeling. As far as working together is concerned, at best we get back alive."

Colin was taut, like a sprung bow. "Maybe you don't want to trust me; I can live with that. Maybe you hate me. But I have concerns too. If I can't rely on you, if I can't trust you, then I go on this mission alone."

The words had a shocking effect. Jack looked stung, then frustration, and anger, flooded his face and he took a step forward. "You dare!" he screeched. "You just dare! We made a deal. You fail me and I'll publish. I swear!"

Colin waved him to be silent. "You got this far, Jack, because you were pitied and because it was thought you might be useful. But don't push it. Do you really believe that if your interests didn't coincide exactly with those of the authorities you'd be here now? Forget it. And if you make enough of a nuisance of yourself they'll shut you down too, and that'll be another waste." His expression softened. "Don't make them shut you down."

A growl, begun deep within Jack's chest, rose like a gusher and burst from him. He charged, murder in his eyes. He swung a fist, but his anger made him clumsy and Colin easily deflected the blow. They progressed across the floor, Jack swinging, grunting with each wild effort, Colin skillfully defending himself. He was surprised at Jack's strength; even allowing for his fury, the punches were not poor. Evidently he had been trained at some point. Colin concentrated on containing him until he wore out.

"Come on Jack...." he muttered, deflecting a punch with an upward flick of his wrist. "I need to know I can rely on you Jack. Or you don't go. Can I trust you?" He was becoming slightly breathless.

"Can I trust you Jack? Can I trust you...?"

"YES!" Jack screamed at last, his chest heaving with anger. He stopped swinging, closed his eyes and pulled his fists close to his chest in a spasm of despair. "Yes you can trust me!"

Colin let his hands fall to his sides. "Good. We can work together. I'm glad about that, Jack."

Jack was breathing hard through his mouth. "You got your deal, Congreave. I'll be a good boy. But I'm putting you on notice..." he jabbed the air with a finger. "When this is over we settle up. Just you and me. Clear?"

Colin peered into the American's eyes and saw the

fiery embers of loathing. Burt could be contained, but only if there was something for him at the end of it all. An end to justify all the pain.

"Agreed," he said peremptorily.

"Good enough." Jack Burt stormed out.

*

17:

Drinks were not hurried. Seeler, in the company of Culum, Norm Nunny and a gangling white haired, pale skinned youth named Sean, sat around a plain wooden table, much scarred with carved initials and cigarette burns. Under the stark glare from a single bulb they sipped from small tumblers, shadows looming large and distorted on the plain walls. The room was a cellar, a windowless dank cubicle with a proliferation of pungent mould breaking through the cracked plaster. They played cards for matchsticks while they talked, but it was an uncompetitive game, played to keep hands busy while the chat ranged.

Seeler was happy with the pace of the drinking. Men like Culum Strong, though able to handle drink, seldom drank enough to inhibit the reflexes. Readiness was a constant in life. The conversation was a challenge, for he was forced to draw masses of information from memory. The hours of talk he had indulged in with the real Dominic, back in London, paying off. He talked easily, embroidering and adjusting to tell the stories from the relevant viewpoint. At times the talk centred on those lost, on ambushes laid by the SAS, and on the subsequent retaliation by the Provos. At times the talk centred on CORE and upon Seeler himself, whom the men knew only by reputation, and his blood ran cold at the depth of knowledge they had about the operations he had been involved in, and the fates planned for him if he should ever fall into the hands of the group.

"Congreave's the one I want." muttered Culum, after explaining to Dominic the details of Mary's death. "I live just to rip that bastard to pieces. I'll feed him his liver."

He was staring hard into his glass. His eyes shone sadly.

The others exchanged glances, and Seeler, intercepting those glances, sensed that Culum was a powder keg when loaded with alcohol.

But Culum drank less as night wore on. He wanted to impress Dominic and was excessively polite and deferrent. Seeler wondered about this for a while until the reality of the situation exploded in his mind. Of course! Dominic was returning from Libya a legend, a man of formidable reputation, and Culum, viewing him as a potential rival, wanted him as an ally! Had he been in less intense company he might have chuckled; the idea of a British secret service agent leading a section of the IRA was preposterous enough to be hysterical. The image of him leading Culum's ASU into the cellars and throwing away the key had a certain appeal.

Inevitably the talk turned to actions planned, and here the dialogue became guarded. Compartmentalisation of offensive strategies had become a strength of the IRA. After a particularly patriotic and almost poetic speech by Culum, his voice resonant with melancholy and pride, the little group rose as one and followed him into a deeper, danker cellar where cases of weapons were stacked on one side and cases of ammunition on the other. Three trestle tables occupied the centre of the floor, and on them were piled small brickshaped packets wrapped in thick, greased paper.

Seeler recognised the packaging immediately. He loosed a low whistle. "Jaysus, there must be six hundred pounds of it."

"Nine hundred." Culum rejoined. His tone was spiced with defiant pride. He walked around the tables at an idle pace, running fingers gently over the packaged bricks as if admiring a work of art, as if drawing inspiration from the deadly potential amassed there.

"Semtex. Grade-A explosive. All ready for our biggest ever strike on the Brits."

Seeler was careful not to voice any of the dozen questions that shot to mind. The entire charade depended on the cell members coming to him. There was no space for him to worm his way in. Safety lay in being embraced.

Culum went on: "We begin shipping it to the mainland next week. We have a container truck going over, packed with legitimate merchandise, with these beauties concealed in the hollow walls of the container. In one month's time we will be ready to launch our fiercest campaign yet."

"What's it to be?" Norm could not resist it - the question popped out like a cork from a champagne bottle. His impetuosity earned him a scowl from Culum, but the leader was ready to tell and his face cleared.

"The politico's are deadlocked with the bastards in Westminster. In the past our attacks on the mainland have only hardened public opinion against us, and the political backlash has made it impossible for our voices to be heard in Westminster. So we tried the political solution. We listened to the boys in the front and relied on lobbying and the ballot box to make our point. Things looked promising for a while, but now we have reached the point where the British are not willing to go any further. Leaving us in limbo. Our boys have walked the halls and talked the talk; still with no result. This leaves the cause divided between those who want the talking to continue and those who want to remind the Brits just how serious we are. It is for this reason the Semtex has been collected here. In one month's time, the Brits will be warned, if further political openings do not appear, we resume the war on the mainland."

"Christmas. The busiest shopping week of the year in London. In London, in the space of a single hour, four one-hundred pound bombs will explode at key points in London. Oxford street, Regent street, Piccadilly Circus and a famous store - again. Designed to create total havoc. And then, on New Year's Eve, five hundred pounds placed in Trafalgar Square will show we are operating on an entirely new scale. There will be seventy thousand people in the square. W'ell wipe out hundreds."

The silence that descended on the group was one of awe. The scale of it, the effect! Seeler's reaction was cold, blind anger, but he controlled it. His mind suddenly changed gear. He had a schedule now; a matter of days. Before the explosive was shifted he would have to move. He felt comfortable with a timetable. From that moment onwards every thought would be directed towards spoiling the plans.

The chill seemed to sharpen. Norm consulted his watch and muttered something about dawn, and they retired to the rooms allocated to them. Seeler threw his bag onto the camp bed prepared for him, and washed in the basin. The water was cold, and after he had washed he studied himself in the jagged triangular piece of mirror tacked by it's apex to the wall. His hair was dyed red, but by parting it and examining the roots he could see the natural dark colour growing through. He had a tiny phial of dye concealed in the lining of his bag. Now he vigorously rubbed a palmful into his scalp. Stripping off, he did the same to the thick knotted hair under his arms and at the base of his belly. He was nothing if not thorough. The process took longer than he would have liked, but he was not disturbed, and slid gratefully into bed within the hour.

But his sleep was disturbed by dreams. Nightmares. He was in London and invisible. He ran from person to person, from place to place, but went unseen and unacknowledged by all. He knew the locations of the bombs and ran from one to the next, arriving at each just too late, and being able to do nothing but look around despairingly at the carnage created by the bomb blasts. The bodies, crushed by toppling rubble, speared by flying glass, burned beyond recognition by searing balls of flame. In his dream he screamed at each new horror.

Then he was in Trafalgar Square. It was packed, sardine-tight, and the atmosphere was a carnival of light and song. Then a deep and threatening rumble from the bowels of the earth burst into the open with a blue flash, and a roar that seemed to fill the heavens. He felt the pressure from the shockwave as it thundered over the heads of the crowd. The sky seemed to split as a second explosion filled the air and a chorus of hysterical screams erupted as Nelson's column trembled, tilted, and, finally, toppled upon the trapped thousands, crashing to earth in a cloud of dust, it's fall muffled, cushioned as it was by tons of flesh. The crowd heaved elastically in all directions, then seemed to collapse upon itself in panic as a great, suffocating cloud of stone dust billowed upwards, choking off the mingled screams....

He was on the edge of the crowd. Cold-welded to the spot. Face agape with horror. Then the crowd surged towards him with unstoppable force and he went under, screaming, still invisible and unheard, screaming until he was trampled into pulp.

*

18:

The following days dragged wearily by, and by his own lights Jack Burt only avoided cracking up by hurling himself totally into the training. He ran faster and harder than anyone, spent longer on the range and in the combat room, and retired early each night after a hefty meal and a single pint of beer in the bar.

The few pounds of fat he had been carrying had hardened into well-defined muscle. Solid ridges of it lined his belly and his arms had shaped up nicely. Mostly though he was happiest about his breathing. He was now able to run without becoming breathless, and that, to him, meant progress. Now he itched to be on the hunt.

Contact with Congreave had been minimal, but on the occasions their paths crossed hard words had erupted. Jack was eager to be moving, but Colin insisted he was not ready yet.

Stanley Murdoch had been despatched to Belfast to begin discreet inquiries and to have rooms ready for their arrival.

For Colin there had been one consolation, one distraction. Anne and the kids were safe at PRISM. They had been kept well away from the paying guests. He and Anne had been brought closer together by the fear, and he had come to realise there was nothing he would not do to keep her and the children from harm. He told her about Jack Burt's family and instantly regretted doing so. She became so distressed it was all he could do to keep her from running to Jack to beg forgiveness. She had wept all that night, wept as they made love, and the fact that he was unable to comfort her made him feel more wretched than ever. Then one evening there came a knock on the door.

Shepherding his family into the bedroom he opened the front door to find Jack Burt standing on the threshold. The American peered over Colin's shoulder, into the room beyond, then abruptly brushed past him.

"So," he snapped, "You get this cosy home from home while the rest of us rough it." He roamed, peered into the compact kitchen, his gaze taking in the pile of used dishes, four of everything, on the drainer. He turned, and his face wore a sour expression. "I' m sick of waiting. Sick of excuses. I want to go."

Colin started to say something, but was interrupted by a loud crash from the bedroom. Flashing a furious scowl at Colin, Jack pushed open the bedroom door, and froze. Young Ben had been piecing together a 500 tile jigsaw puzzle on a small table and had accidentally knocked over the whole lot. Now he and his sister stared open-mouthed at the stranger in the doorway. Anne, who was on the floor, scrabbling for the strewn pieces, looked up at him, embarassed, and pushed back a strand of hair that hung before her eyes. She began to rise. "Mr Burt...?"

Jack spun abruptly and glowered at Colin. "You son of a bitch. Quite an act you and Parsons have going here. Had me fooled pretty good, didn't you? You had me out there, running until I dropped, 'til I puked, stalling me, just so you could hang around here with your bitch and her brats!" His voice rose to a roar. "I want to get moving. Do you hear me?"

"I hear you." Colin's nostrils flared as his own fury ignited. Then he caught sight of Anne, leaning weakly against the door jamb, and saw the pain in her eyes. He forced his voice down to a taut whisper. "Make out your will. We leave tonight. Now get out before I do something I could be jailed for." His fists shook as he teetered on the brink of losing control. Burt thundered past him, slamming shut the door with a hollow crash. With a cry, Anne ran into Colin's embrace. He rocked her gently until nightfall when, too exhausted by crying to stay awake, she lapsed into fitful slumber.

At the kitchen table he sat down to compose a note. He tried to keep it simple and lighthearted - be back before you know it. But somehow he knew she would read between the lines and know this was the most dangerous mission he had yet undertaken. This time it was personal, and personal involvement in any mission clouds a man's judgement.

There had never been a greater probability of him not coming back.

Folding the note he stood it against a vase of flowers on the table. Then he crept into the bedroom. She looked radiant. Moonlight, sifting in through lace curtains, bathed her face in soft light. Looking at her, and knowing the risks he was about to run, he felt something tug at his heart. He knelt beside her and gently kissed her forehead. She murmured, moved slightly. "Colin...?"

"Sleep, honey," he whispered, and saw her lips form a half smile. "Sleep. Sweet dreams."

He stood, and moved stealthily to the door, halting as she softly called his name once more.

"What is it?" he whispered.

"I love you."

He took a breath; it was going to be hard to leave. Sudden sadness swamped him, and he felt with utter surety that he would not be returning.

"Same here," he replied. Then swallowing manfully, he crept out into the night.

Parsons had his Range Rover ready. He was going to drive the two men to Holyhead, from where they meant to take a ferry. As Colin ran out to the vehicle with his hastily packed case, the night over the camp was dense, the powerful headlamp beams rendered almost inneffectual. They followed a winding lane into the mountains, Colin looking back until sight of the camp was lost to him. Then he turned his eyes to the road ahead. He was nervous, more so than ever before.

Parsons shot him a glance. Clear eyes glinting astutely as he studied his old friend's face. "You okay?"

Colin forced his expression to harden. "I'm alright." he growled. "Let's do it."

*

19:

Finnbar Craig had the wild-eyed look of a man on the road too long. His hair, a mass of black, unruly curls, swirled about his head as he walked with a stiff, jerky movement. Intense. His shoulders were hunched, and the collar of his thin green fatigues jacket was turned up against the wind. He wore crumpled, stained trainers and patchworked corduroy pants. As he walked, with hands tucked into pockets, he regularly darted glances over his shoulder.

He had been on the run since the age of sixteen. Since he first killed a man.

The windows of the T-Bar coffee room were steamed up and impenetrable. He pulled open the door and ducked inside, his body shuddering slightly as the humid air took the chill off him. The proprietor made a fuss of him, hurrying to the counter with a mug of tea and biscuits, but Finnbar was not fooled. Like everyone else the man hated and feared him, but elected to take the safest course and pander to him. They were all the same, Finnbar reminded himself. Wanted the Brits out, were happy to sit back and let others, like himself and Culum, put their lives on the line for the cause. When all along they were scared shitless. He poured sugar into the steaming mug, then stared pointedly at the proprietor. The man, with gesturing eyebrows and a movement of his head, conveyed the message that the man Finnbar sought was in a corner of the tea room.

Finn turned slowly to survey the room. The proprietor edged neared and whispered into his ear. "That's the one. He was asking about you." he gulped, nervously. "I thought you'd want to know."

The man hovered, craving recognition, and Finn obliged with a tiny shift of his head that might have meant a dozen things.

The proprietor retired into his back kitchen, gratified.

There was no one in the place that Finn knew. Rapidly he gauged the few occupants at the formica topped tables. There was the cripple in the wheelchair, being spoonfed tea by his fat old mammy and still managing to drool most of it down his greasy overcoat. The old man with dandruff-spotted grey hair, his gnarled hands hooked around a cup that would take him half a day to finish. The young mother, three shrieking kids around her and another swelling her belly beneath her worn coat. Poor slag, listening to the Priests! They never had to put up with dropping babies like flies. Her clothing was poor and her hair, falling in irregular waves to her shoulders, was in need of a trim. But her face was the classical colleen sculpture; nicely rounded, cheeks well scrubbed, dark eyes strong despite the cares heaped upon her by life. Finn considered dragging her into the back. He was like that. All the better if she struggled. He loved it when they struggled. Not for him the staying true and the heartache friend Culum had endured over Mary. He took it when he wanted it.

In one corner a middleaged couple argued in low, shrewish tones, and he guessed that the man was coming off worst. That just left the man in the opposite corner, the one the proprietor had called him about. The one who asked questions. He was large built and wore a trenchcoat, and he appeared engrossed in a newspaper. Finn sensed he was not concentrating on the newsprint. This was a man who seldom relaxed. He might have been a cop, but if he was he was not from around here. Not quite.

Taking his mug, Finn wandered over to the corner and took the seat opposite trenchcoat. Taking out a crumpled pack of cigarettes he lit one and settled back on his seat. His gaze aimed steadily at the man behind the newspaper.

Then without warning, Finn said: "I hear you've been looking for somboddy. A Mr Craig."

Trenchcoat emerged from behind the paper. His eyes met Finn's gaze, and the Irishman spotted the flickering unease that told him the stranger was out of his depth. Finnbar felt confident. "I may be able to help you." he said. "For a price."

Trenchcoat narrowed his eyes. He lowered the newspaper. He was not to be taken in THAT easily. He had been extremely unhappy about coming to Belfast. He knew, better than Jack Burt did, the dangers inherent in asking questions about the Provos in and around the Catholic areas. He had been nervous, approaching two or three likely names he had been given by former colleagues in The Met. Through these names he had been told the best chance he had of finding information on the man he sought was to let slip remarks in two or three bars. At first, self consciously, he had fudged, and fled the bars in nervous panic, wondering what on earth he was doing, getting this involved. But then he had struck lucky, hit a conversational tack that led him to this cafe. If he let it be known here, it was said, either Culum Strong or Finnbar Craig or someone who knew them, would find him.

Now he was faced by this wild-haired youth, lean and crazy looking, arrogantly puffing smoke at him and grinning like he was in on some secret. Trenchcoat cleared his throat, and assumed a poker face; it was time to bargain.
"Why would you want to do that?"

Finn sucked on his cigarette, held the smoke in his mouth for what seemed an age, then blew it out again. Insolently. "Let's say I'm no lover of the man." He grinned, and it was the grin that did it. Trenchcoat read something there and misinterpreted. The paper went down and so did his guard. He was sold. "When can you take me to him?"

The cigarette moved jerkily at the corner of his mouth as Finnbar smirked.
"Just as soon as we've talked terms."

*

20:

They arrived in Holyhead late morning. The wind had whipped up to fifty miles an hour, and the ferry sailing they hoped to be on was cancelled, leaving them with a day to kill. Taking a twin room in the North Euston Hotel, overlooking the pounding ocean, they left their cases and went down to the lobby bar for a last drink with Parsons.

Even though little was said, the emnity between Congreave and Burt set the air alight. Finally Parsons, tiring of the stilted formality, put down his glass.

"Listen you two. You have to come to terms with each other if you want to win this one. Colin, you've always been coolheaded, lead the way. And you, Jack, respect Colin's judgement. He's a good man to have covering your back. Come on. Shape up."

If he had expected some revelation, a sudden outpouring of friendship, he was to be disappointed. Neither man spoke. No handshake was offered. Parsons impatiently swallowed his drink and stood to go. They followed him outside, and the wind lashed at him as they exchanged final pleasantries.

Colin stuck out his hand and felt Parsons' large grasp close around it. "Take care of them for me, Dave." He almost choked on the words.

"Bank on it." Parsons replied. Then he smiled, and the sight of him standing there, tall and strong and honest, with the wind tousling his hair and his bright eyes sparkling, was the way Colin would always think of him. Parsons shook hands with Jack, then he was in his car and reversing into a tight turn before driving away.

The two looked at each other. Jack appeared restless, seemed reluctant to return indoors. "Listen," he began, evasively, "I'm gonna take a walk. Maybe find us a later sailing today. Why the hell we couldn't fly I'll never know. You alright?" he asked Colin, almost as an afterthought.

Colin nodded. "Yes. I'll get a paper and see you in the lounge. You know, we've already paid for the room. If you get us on to a sailing today we can't claim a refund."

Jack responded with a sardonic smirk. "It's okay. My treat." He turned away and sauntered down the shorefront.

One hour later he walked up to Congreave in the lounge and threw a paper wallet onto the table next to Colin's drink. "Four thirty sailing." He said, simply. "I'll bring down the bags."

*

21:

Evening was drawing in when Seeler awoke to the realisation that he was aching from head to toe. The camp bed with it's defeated springs had sagged badly under his weight, and he had slept at a peculiar angle. He groaned loudly on standing, then splashed himself awake at the basin.

The smell of cooking, plain but inviting, filled the corridors of the old house as he neared the kitchen. He found the others seated around a circular table, tucking into deep bowls filled with stew. Irish stew; he chuckled to himself as he took his seat. But he was famished, and his mouth watered as Culum himself filled the big man's bowl. There were thick slices of cut bread piled on a plate and he went to with a will, mopping clean his dish and settling back with a satisfied sigh. "Compliments to the chef, Culum. Was it yourself?"

"No, Norm." Culum smiled, and for the first Seeler saw the smile extend to the man's eyes. They flashed black.

"You're a talented man, Norm." Seeler beamed. Norm blushed. Somewhere in the house a telephone rang. Sean, who was lean and white headed, gaunt cheeked and with eyes of arctic blue, slid from his chair and glided out of the room. Watching him leave, Seeler remarked on the way he walked; smoothly. Norm replied: "He's one of these karatee people. He went to one of those Jappo countries to learn how to walk as if his head is touching the ceiling. Some crap like that."

"Centre of gravity and discipline," Culum added. "Stand right, walk right, fight right."

The telephone had stopped ringing. In his mind Seeler tried to place it's location - he might need to reach it in a hurry. Then he heard the ding of a bell as the receiver was slammed down, closely followed by the slap of feet running on hard flooring. When Sean burst into the kitchen he looked disturbed and excited. "That was Finnbar. There's trouble. He'll be bringing in a prisoner."

The others stared at him. "Did he say who?" Culum asked. Sean shook his head. "No, but he said to have the botttom cellar ready."

Culum pushed back his chair and got to his feet. "Come on then. We have work to do."

*

Finnbar drove his battered transit van into the courtyard and reversed to the garage door. He clambered out with the force of a whirlwind, greeted Culum, barely acknowledged Sean and Norm and gave Dominic no more than the fleetest glance. Then the back door was opened and they were carrying a struggling, bound man with a hood over his head, into the bottom cellar. This was a small, dank cubicle equipped with a sinister workbench and a heavy chair fitted with restraining straps. The prisoner was lowered into the chair, unbound and strapped in, before the hood was removed from his head. His face, when it emerged, was flushed red with anger and fear.

Stanley Murdoch looked around at his captors and felt a fear, a terror, greater than anything he had ever known in his life. He tried to hold himself together, but he couldn't, he couldn't.....

Finnbar circled in a predatory manner, and Norm, in a moment of untypical animation, cried out: "Hey look! He's pissing himself!" The others joined Norm in laughter as the dark stain spread down the leg of Murdoch's pale trousers.

Culum looked at Finnbar. "What's going on?"

Finn wiped a calloused hand across his mouth. "He's been asking questions. About you. About me. At first I thought he might be a cop, but if he is he's either not from around here or he's green as grass. I thought we might benefit from a chat."

Moving to the workbench, he picked up a heavy electric drill connected to the mains supply. He gave the trigger an experimental squeeze. The bit whirred hungrily, then died. The prisoner let out a tiny whimper. Finnbar fixed his wild gaze on Seeler, as though seeing him for the first time. "So, this is Dominic, eh? I've heard a lot about you."

Seeler calmly returned the stare. Unlike his first meeting with Culum, he did not offer to shake hands. He sensed that with Finnbar, this would be taken as a sign of weakness; yielding first. His mind though, was also juggling with other problems. Who knew where this prisoner had come from, or what he knew?

Finnbar swaggered nearer to the prisoner, the drill held at a tilt like any handgun. Murdoch's petrified gaze stayed locked on the bit.

"Well, Dominic," Finn challenged with deadly arrogance. "Do you remember how to kneecap?" He held out the drill.

With a shrill cry, Murdoch fainted.

At the exact moment Stanley Murdoch tightened every muscle in terror as he prepared - if one ever really COULD prepare - for the touch of the spinning drill, as he pulled against the restraining straps, his teeth gritted and his jaw clamped tight, Congreave and Burt were arriving at the hotel Murdoch had booked for them. And at the moment Murdoch burst out screaming, blood gurgling at the back of his throat, Congreave signed the register.

"I can't understand Stan not being here." Burt said. Congreave shrugged. "He could be following a lead and didn't want to risk losing it. We can take care of ourselves. Maybe he couldn't get away."

Murdoch's head jerked back as he screamed at the ceiling. The muscles in his neck bulged like straining whipcord, and his fists shook violently in the straps. He bit down hard on his tongue and felt blood flow into his mouth.

They went down to the restaurant and ordered drinks while they scanned the menu. Conversation was still difficult, but they went through the motions. Jack fidgeted on his seat, toyed with the drink in his hand. "I don't feel right about Murdoch. He's so reliable - it's a vice with him. He would have been here."

Congreave shrugged. "We'll give him until morning to show. Who knows? Maybe he's fallen for a local skirt." He grinned at his own joke, but inwardly he was as concerned as Burt. Murdoch had not been able to turn up, Instinct told him and he had long ago learned to rely on instinct. That had been one of the things Seeler pounded into him years ago; overlook nothing.

Jack Burt was correct to be concerned, and Colin determined to be ready for anything that might happen in the night.

They delayed over dinner, then sat in the bar engaging in

desultory conversation until it closed. Most of the hotel had shut down. Only a plump, grimfaced porter, reading a girlie magazine in a cubicle off reception, was available.

"Colin," Jack said in a gentle stage whisper. "Keep the porter busy for a few minutes, will you? I want to take a few precautions."

Congreave smiled: "Great minds! If you hadn't suggested it, I would have. I'll book us a morning call. Tea, continental breakfast and papers. Mine's The Telegraph what's yours?"

"Give him something to think about," Jack grinned. "Ask him for USA Today."

Colin leapt up and walked to the cubicle. He leaned inside, obscuring the porter's view, and Jack heard his voice as he loudly placed the order.

Jack hurried nimbly around the other side of the reception desk and scanned the room occupation board, showing which rooms were allocated to which guests. It took him only a few seconds to roughly work out the system, select a vacant room and pocket the key from a bank of pigeon holes. Then making for the cubicle he squeezed into the hatch beside Colin and addressed the porter in his broadest yankee accent. "Hey, buddy, do you think you can get me what I want?"

The porter assured him it ought to be no problem. Wishing them goodnight, he went back to the magazine.

"Which room are we in now?" Colin muttered through the corner of his mouth as they approached the stairs.

"Seventy one." Jack told him. "All we have to do is make sure we get back to our own room in time for the morning call."

The work was done. When he put down the drill, Finnbar was breathing heavily. The grip was smeared vivid red. He swallowed, and his voice was guttural with subsiding excitement. "Get me whiskey, somebody."

"I'll go." Seeler volunteered. "I want to take a leak anyway." He turned through the door before anything could be said. He had to get to the telephone. Call the hotel and warn Congreave. Christ! Talk about coming home to roost! Congreave in Belfast to hit Culum and Finnbar, and now the two irishmen knew about it. And who was this other man, Jack Burt? Family massacred, IRA blamed? When Murdoch dribbled out the story, about the blood-smeared walls and the word, MARY, Culum and Finnbar had exchanged looks and grown strangely quiet. They finished off Murdoch soon afterwards.

He found the whisky on a cupboard top, and, by a stroke of luck, found the telephone in the same room. A well used directory lay on a shelf. Taking it down he thumbed through the soft pages, quickly finding the number of the hotel. He dialled.

The night operator on the hotel switchboard tried the room repeatedly, then returned to Seeler who was impatiently switching his weight from one foot to the other.

"I'm sorry, sir, but there's no reply. Yes, I'm sure I have the correct room. The two gentlemen are sharing. Any message? Goodnight then Sir."

Seeler carried the bottle and five tumblers back to the cellar. The body had been removed but the chair stood there, an ominous reminder. Seeler wondered how often it had been used.

Generous measures were poured, drained, and refills taken. Then Finnbar remarked to Culum; "We have things to talk about." and the smaller man nodded glumly.

Of all the group, Sean seemed the least affected - at least outwardly. Norm looked decidedly green. For Seeler, to whom torture was a hated territory, the entire experience had been unpleasant, and he struggled to keep distaste from his face. At one point Finnbar, angered by Dominic's lack of relish for the grisly task, had shouldered the big man aside. "Back off. Let a man in," he cried. His face was speckled with flecks of blood. His eyes blazed madly.

And Murdoch had screamed. And grovelled. And pleaded. And told all.

Culum left the room, Finnbar close behind him. At the door Finn spun around and snapped: "Get this mess cleaned up." Then he too was gone, and the three remaining shared the dreadful peace. The floor was cambered, and scarlet rivulets, oddly livid in the glare from the unshaded bulb, trailed in all directions down the slope, collecting in narrow channels and trickling into drain holes at each corner.

"I'll get a bucket of water." Norm muttered, looking sick. He hastened away, taking care not to tread in the blood.

Sean was bloody from carrying out the body. He leaned against the wall and nonchalantly sipped at his whiskey. His eyes were vacant, misty, as though daydreaming.

Seeler looked around him, eyed the bloody trails, smelt the abattoir tang, and muttered, "Jaysus, what a mess."

*

22:

Dawn.

Seeler viewed the onset of the new day through a grimy window. The deep of night yielded to the glow of the dawn sun, fanning upwards over the horizon. The cold power of the morning sun brought no warmth, and the big man shivered. His brain was fogged with fatigue, and his eyelids itched as if lined with sand. He was tensely aware that he had never been in a tighter spot. Right at the heart of the enemy camp he had to plot and counterplot. Play both sides and still emerge with his skin intact.

Seated opposite him across the table, Sean sat with his hands clasped loosely on his lap. His eyes were closed and his breathing sonorous and even. Culum and Finnbar had spent hours arguing, with their heads together at the end of the long table. In bouts of furious recrimination since emerging from their private meeting the previous night, Finnbar had tried to browbeat his friend. Culum was a simple man at heart - he wanted revenge, but the simplest possible. Finnbar though was slyer than any fox, and revelled in cruelty. He wanted to lure Congreave, to trap, terrorise and, finally, despatch him in as gory and as undignified a fashion imaginable. His fervency was wearing Culum down, and Seeler feared for Congreave if events went Finnbar's way.

Fatigue and vitriol made Finnbar even more wildeyed, and the monochrome steeping of pale light and deep shade gave his features a glowing, sepulchral hardness, an unfeeling stone fixedness.

"Listen, Culum lad." His voice wore on, grindingly persuasive. "Trust me on this. Back in France I promised you revenge. Now let me give it to you. A bullet's too good for that bastard, I want him to pay and pay again." As he spoke, his hand slowly pumped up and down as if driving in a nail. "Stand by me on this and you'll have all the vengeance you want and more."

Culum wearily lifted his gaze. "Finn, that's what I'm afraid of. When it comes to the cause I'm as staunch as the next man..."

Finnbar raised his hands. "I don't doubt that."

"But I don't have the stomach you have for...."Culum struggled for the right words. "...imaginative revenge. I prefer a clean shot."

Finnbar leapt to his feet. "After what he did to you? Come on man!"

"A clean shot, Finn. Then on with life!"

With a snort of disgust Finn dropped back onto his seat. He struggled visibly for control, one moment teetering on the brink of violence, the next, pulling on the reins. At last he settled. He went to work on Culum in a voice that was silk soft, relentlessly probing for a weakness he could exploit.

"Have you forgotten your anger that day, brother? Have you forgotten it was Finn who was with you as you watched that sweet girl die? Can you just forgive and forget? What would she have done for you?" The smile on his face quivered, became one almost of triumph. He had focused on Culum's weak spot - his guilt - and pushed.

"She would have died for me." Culum growled. "Don't do this, Finn."

But his friend was not one to stop half way. The needle was in, now he wanted to push it through and loop it back in an immovable stitch. He leaned forward, and even watching from a distance Seeler could feel the heat of his intensity. "Yes, Cully, she would have died for you. She would have gone in with that little knife of hers and taken him apart piece by piece. Can't you do more for her than a clean shot?" he put out a hand that enclasped Culum's fingers. "Forget the remote control, Cully. Get in close, let them feel your power. For her sake ---"

"Alright!" Culum screamed, snatching his hand free. "Alright. Set it up. I'll be ready when you are." Kicking aside his chair he boomed out. They heard the clattering of his boots in the corridor.

Norm appeared in the doorway and halted, unsure, on the threshold. Finnbar glanced at him, then said: "Make us some coffee, eh Norm? And put a stiffener in it."

Norm reappeared minutes later with a tray upon which sat coffee pot and cups, and a brace of whiskey bottles. Finnbar liberally topped up each cup as it was emptied. He was twitchy, and Seeler, sensing that something dangerously impulsive lurked beneath the Irishman's brooding exterior, adopted caution.

As Finnbar drank he began to ramble. His words loose, verging on incoherence. They were also personal. Sneering. Norm shuffled uneasily on his seat. He was a good and loyal follower, but hated to get in too close; there were things he would rather not know. Sean mused languidly, posing, his cup suspended between spanned fingers.

Seeler drank in controlled measures. He kept himself very still. Better to let Finnbar expend whatever insane energy drove him.

"It'll do Culum good, getting rid of Congreave. He's not been the same man since Mary was blown away." He chuckled, an eerie sound in the half light of dawn.

Seeler had been hoping Finn would tire and go to bed, but as light flooded in, making Finn look flesh and blood again, his spirits seemed to rise and he grew restless to be moving. "Norm," he barked. "Get pen and paper. Let's put down all we can remember about that bastard's confessions while they're still fresh in our minds. It's time to plan."

Jack Burt entered the hotel restaurant and joined Colin at the breakfast table. "I've ordered," Colin told him. "Egg and bacon okay?"

Jack nodded absently. He was frowning, his brows beetled. "Murdoch's not back yet, but listen to this; we had a call in the night. Of course it went to our empty room."

Colin broke open a croissant and began to smother the centre with butter. "No message?"

Jack shook his head. "It could have been any of a number of things. Murdoch calling to let us know where he was..."

"Or the bad guys checking to see if we were in before hitting us." Colin said around a mouthful.

"How long do we give him?"

Colin pondered for a moment. "We'll give him the day. Then we begin our own enquiries." Taking another bite from the croissant, he chewed thoughtfully, then gulped coffee. "After breakfast, maybe we should take a peek in Stanley's room."

The corridor was deserted. Halting outside Murdoch's door, Colin took a penknife from a pocket. He opened the knife to reveal an assortment of blades, most of them not standard. "What are those?" Jack asked him, intrigued. "Picks?"

Eyeing the lock, Colin shook his head. "No. Picks are good, but if you are stopped by the police for some reason they can't really be mistaken for anything else. But a penknife is the sort of thing you could find in almost any pocket. And once the blades have been modified slightly, they work just as well." Selecting a wafer-thin, slightly curved blade he slotted it into the lock. He worked it gently for a moment, then gave a sudden jerk. The door fell open under his weight.

Jack followed him into the room and shut the door. "I'm impressed."

While he watched, Colin methodically and expertly searched the room. When he had finished the place looked exactly as it had before he began.

"Struck out again." Jack said glumly. Colin nodded. "Let's go see the town."

As they crossed the lobby they were hailed by the day porter. The man hurried towards them, a newspaper in hand. "Here you are, Sir." he gasped, thrusting the paper at Jack. "USA Today."

Jack and Colin exchanged glances, and burst into involuntary laughter. "That's terrific," Jack said to the porter, tipping him a couple of pounds. "Thank you. Thank you very much."

As they turned for the door Colin was hailed by a male receptionist in a neat morning suit. "Message for you Sir."

Colin took the message, read it, and a smile creased his face. "It's from Murdoch." he told Jack. "He's fine. He'll be back tomorrow with some news."

Finnbar told the others what he had done. They listened in blank silence. "That ought to take their minds of the late Mr Murdoch." Finn chuckled. "While they stay put, waiting for him to turn up, we'll go into town and size them up. Then, Culum my friend..." He slapped Culum on the back. "You'll have your revenge."

Culum raised a thin smile, then got up and left the group. Finn glanced around, at Sean and Dominic at the table, and Norm, elbow deep in suds at the sink. "When you're done there, Norm, break out the weapons. We've some trapping to do."

*

23:

Evening.

"Hello Anne, how are you love?" Colin greeted his wife over the telephone. "I'm fine. How are the kids?"

Jack Burt was on the bed, perched upright against bunched pillows, making a concerted effort to read a book. He did not want to overhear the conversation, but could not avoid it. Just as he did not want to think about the past, and could not suppress the bitterness once the past thoughts had been triggered. Being in Belfast had made the bad times seem a world away, and he had even begun to grow used to Congreave, but now waves of anger swept over him, and the grief was potent enough to make him reel.

Finally he could bear it no longer. Rolling off the bed and onto his feet he stormed out and headed for the elevator.

The lobby was quiet, no telephones ringing, no bustle. At the desk two young females were engaged in quiet industry. The night porter was back on duty, light winking off his sheeny bald head as he pored over a magazine. Restless, Jack strolled out through the front entrance and paused atop the steps.

A light drizzle had dampened the pavement, and the glow from the streetlamps shimmered fuzzily. Traffic was light. Cars were parked along both sides of the street. Jack, using an awareness ignored since his days in the steamy jungles of Vietnam, scanned the street. Unease had been needling at him for hours. He was positive Congreave felt the same, but neither had spoken of it.

He clenched a fist. Secretly he harboured the hope that he might get away from Congreave, face Culum Strong alone. He wanted to put a gun to the man's head. Wanted to see the expression on the Irishman's face as his brains were blown out.

A dark van, parked some fifty metres away, held his attention, then the hotel doors were pushed open behind him and he was distracted by the sound.

"How are you feeling?" Colin asked him.

Inexplicably, Jack felt tears sting his eyes. His mind was suddenly filled with recollections; the happy times, and he choked back a sob. "I'm fine," he replied, keeping his head averted until he was sure of his control.

"Jack, I haven't forgotten either. Believe me, we'll get them."

Inside the van, Finnbar leaned forward and peered through the winscreen, eyes straining to make out the two men on the steps at the hotel entrance. He hissed: "What d'ye think, Cully. Is it them?"

Culum was visibly trembling. His eyes glowered through the gloom, straining for a spark of recognition. "Blast it. I think so but ----Aw, fuck it. I can't be dead sure from here."

Finn gave a hollow laugh. "And me and you can't chance going in. We might be recognised, and that could spoil things." He glanced around at the others, seated uncomfortably in the dark rear of the van. "Young Sean," he said after a pause designed to keep them on edge. "You've a level head on you. Go in and see if you can't get the names of those two men."

Sean looked uncomfortable. "But Finnbar, how do I do that?"

"Initiative, lad. Time you learned to think on your feet. You going, or what?" Sean looked no less at ease, but he nodded. He was willing to do almost anything to be accepted.

He knew his time to be tested - really tested, was coming. He steeled himself.

Sensing a number of possibilities, Seeler chipped in with an idea. "Speak to them if you can. Spin a yarn - tell them you come from Murdoch. Try to find out which rooms they're in."

"Good idea, Dominic." Culum said. Seeing the expression of uncertainty on Sean's face, he winked. "Come on lad, it'll be good experience for you."

Finnbar eyed Seeler with curious arrogance. As though he wanted to hold the big man in contempt, but was not sure he could get away with it. "Yeah," he echoed Culum's praise. "Good thinking big feller."

Sean spoke then, and Seeler could have hugged the man. "Why not have Dominic there to back me in case something goes wrong? We know he can handle it."

Finnbar swallowed; he wanted to deny the big man any opportunity to prove leadership. There was something about Dominic that disquieted him. The man was freelance, and could not be trusted. He preferred those more fervent in their devotion to the cause. Still, he had come with the highest of recomendations - that of Dessi O'Bain. He reluctantly agreed to Sean's request.

Seeler and Sean slipped from the shadow of the van and crossed the street. They sauntered, as though out for an evening stroll, though they did not look dressed for it. As they mounted the steps Seeler felt the rush of adrenalin. He was battle ready.

The lobby was deserted save the receptionist. Sean muttered a curse, but Seeler marched boldly up to the desk and asked to speak to messrs Congreave and Burt. The girl at the desk glanced around: "They were just here, Sir. Just a moment, I'll have them paged." She vanished into a backroom. Sean positioned himself some yards away. Though he tried hard to hide it, his nervousness shone through. Seeler guessed, correctly, that this was something new to the lad, and he felt comforted; it ought to be easy to control the situation.

A tannoy'd message rang through the building. The receptionist reappeared. "If they are still in the building they should hear the page."

Thanking her, Seeler joined Sean. "Jaysus," snapped the younger man. "Why'd you do that?"

Seeler smiled calmly. "Relax. we want a good look at them, don't we?" But Sean was not comforted. A moment later he stiffened. "Look!" he hissed.

A tall, muscularly built man emerged from the adjacent lounge. His eyes scanned the lobby, settling warily on Seeler and Sean. Another man appeared behind him.

Colin followed Jack out of the lounge. He saw Jack's head turning as he looked around. He sensed, rather than saw, him stiffen as he approached the pair of rough looking men standing near the desk. On seeing them, Colin primed himself. Sizing up the two, he decided that the larger of the two was the more dangerous. There was just something about him.

"Wait here," Seeler muttered out of the corner of his mouth. He stepped forward and spoke to the two men approaching. "Mr Congreave, Mr Burt?"

"I'm Congreave." said Colin, arriving at Jack's side."What can we do for you?" His eyes narrowed as he peered at the big man; Christ, where had he seen him before?

"It's not necessary for you to know who I am. I'm just here to bring you a message from Mr Murdoch."

Seeler! The thought exploded in Colin's mind. Though his expression remained wary, inside of him excitement surged. Glancing around, as if fearing they might be overheard, he said loudly: "In that case, you better come over here." He led the way to a corner.

Sean studied them from the desk. Secretly he was glad to be out of it. Hiding his fear behind arrogance, he adopted an aggressively nonchalant stance, leaning against the reception desk with his arms crossed.

There was not the time for introductions or interruptions. Seeler went straight to the point. "Colin, Jack, I haven't much time so listen. Do you understand?" He looked at Congreave.

"I understand." Colin answered for both of them, then half turned to Burt. "This man is a friend, Jack."

The American frowned in puzzlement, but refrained from questions. "Go on." he growled.

"Murdoch is dead. He was was tortured by Culum and Finnbar. They know you're here and they plan to hit you, probably in the next day or so. I'll do what I can, but you'll have to be prepared. Now, I want you to contact the local SAS contingent. Speak to a Colonel Philips. Tell him I've been in touch, and that tonight I'll have the transmitter on. Maybe we can mop up the ASU I'm in with at one fell swoop."

Congreave asked him if he wanted the army to go in as support. Seeler wasn't sure. "It would be nice to take them all, but the place has to be properly reconnoiterd first. They have nine hundred pounds of Semtex stockpiled."

Burt loosed a low whistle. Seeler straightened. "I'm out of time. I have to be going."

As he turned away to rejoin Sean, Burt played the role and grasped him by the sleeve. In a loud and impatient voice he said: "Tell Murdoch I'm getting tired of waiting."

Seeler nodded his shaggy head. Rejoining Sean, he turned for the door. As they reached the step, the young man touched

Seeler on the arm to stall him. "I was nervous, Dominic."

Seeler turned his grey eyes upon him and smiled reassuringly. "I know. I understand that. Action in the gym is one thing. Reality can be quite a differnet proposition."

Sean reared, almost as if stung. "I'm no coward. I would have been there for you. It's just...."

Seeler put up a hand. "Really, I do know that. I'm a good judge of men. I know you'll come through alright. You just need that first taste."

Sean sighed with relief. He had been afraid the big man would sneer.

"I had a first time too." Seeler told him. So don't worry. I won't say anything to the others. Just fall in line with what I say." He paused, smiled. Sean smiled back.

"Come on," said the big man. "We better be getting back."

"How did it go?" Finnbar demanded eagerly the moment they were back in the van. The engine roared into life, and in moments they were moving, taking a corner.

"It went fine." Sean told him. He was looking confident again. "We found them. I'll Let Dominic tell you."

In the gloom Seeler smiled.

*

24:

If Culum was pleased at Seeler's telling, Finnbar was ecstatic. He shook his fists in the air. "Brilliant! They'll be sitting ducks!"

Seeler told them Murdoch was bringing a vital witness forward, someone who 'Knew the way to Culum.' That was his explanation. "They'll stay put," he said, noting with satisfaction the looks of total belief on the faces of the others. Sean, grateful to have come through with his reputation intact, his lack of confidence still to be discovered, was fulsome in his praise for Dominic. Finnbar grew silent as he listened, but finally had to admit, grudgingly, that the big man had done a good job.

It was close to midnight when they drew near to the farm. There were vehicles parked in the yard, and Finnbar, recognising one of them, muttered a curse. "Company."

"That's Connor's car," said Culum. Turning, he spoke over his shoulder to Sean and Seeler. "Brigade Chief Connor Black. It's rare he comes into the open. It's an honour."

"He'll have Seamus O'Toole with him. These days he's always popping up around Connor." Finnbar chimed in sourly. "Fancies himself a politician these days."

"The London Campaign is their baby." Culum reminded him.

Once indoors they were greeted by figures emerging from the shadows. All the lights were out, but Seeler could make out a dozen men, four with automatic weapons in their hands. Once identities were established, the weapons were slung, introductions effected, and the group convened in the kitchen where hot drinks were handed out.

Connor was a sallow faced man with vast shoulder. He

shook Seeler's hand, and though his grip was vice-like, Seeler gained the impression that the man was ill. He was too thin for his size, and the lines on his face were deeply drawn. He had the look of a man who had lost too much weight too fast. Seeler had heard of Connor, his hardness and courage, and he tempered his elation with self regard, for he truly was deep in enemy territory.

The events of the evening were not discussed. Each group operated on a strict need-to-know basis. Connor and his men knew nothing of the plans Finnbar had for Congreave and Burt.

Seamus O'Toole, stout and barrel chested, with a round face and eyes of iron blue,took the centre of the room and addressed the meeting.

"The group has been compromised." This statement was met with a chorus of murmured protest. They all knew each other, and it seemed hard to imagine whom among them could be the hated tout. It had been thought impossible for a leak to exist in this group. O'Toole held up his hands to demand quiet. "I know what you're thinking, but we have to look at the facts. Dessi was sold out. He walked into a trap."

A voice in the crowd rang out: "Seamus, as a group the people in this room have been together for what, two years?"

Seamus's gimlet gaze singled out the man. "All I can tell you is this; we have sources in the RUC, you know that, and if Dessi had walked into a coincidental roadblock we would have heard."

Connor chipped in: "The secrecy that shrouds the details of that particular roadblock is too intense. That has to be because the army were tipped off. No other reason."

Finnbar fixed Seeler with an accusing eye. "There is one newcomer here."

All eyes turned to the big man. He stood unperturbed. It was left for Connor to speak for him. "Dominic may be new to you young fellas, Finnbar, but I've known of him for years. He's been a prime feed for us in the middle east, training our lads, and he's done a fine job. He has nothing to prove as far as I'm concerned, and I had heard he proved himself to you."

Finnbar swallowed his ire and quietly smouldered. Culum tried to break the tension. "So what are you planning?" he asked Seamus.

"We're bringing forward the shipping of the Semtex. We have to get it to safety, onto the mainland and cached. We move first thing in the morning." This news sent a ripple of unease through the gathering. None there relished the idea of moving suddenly, for to do so meant unrealistic risk. They all knew that safety lay in planning.

"Quiet." Seamus spoke tersely, and the men fell silent. "To keep the news from leaking, we all stay indoors tonight."

"Everything has been rearranged." Connor added. "The container is ready and a space on the freighter booked."

"You want us to help you load up?" Finnbar asked him. "And give us armed protection until we are loaded onto the ship."

"We'll be glad to help." Culum assured him. Finnbar interrupted. "Wait a minute, Cully. We have things to do tomorrow." He stared pointedly at his friend, but Culum, relieved secretly to put off the action against Congreave, ignored his appeal. "Finn, we have to put the aims of the cause first. The London initiative is vital."

Finnbar's face narrowed, and his eyes flashed as his anger increased. "They don't need us all."

Seamus stiffened. He stared around the room, then focused

on Finn. They all felt the force of his will as he dominated. "Yes, we do."

The wills of the two clashed, then with a shrug and a slightly embarassed smile, Finn capitulated, and the tension palpable in the room lessened. "Then we're with you, Seamus. Tell us what's to happen."

A heavy earthenware jug of poteen was produced and passed around.

Connor Black cornered Seeler an hour later, and over a drink they talked of aquaintances mutual to both Connor and Dominic. Seeler was cautious. His recollections from his many talks with Dominic himself, back at the cellars, and from the intelligence files, were still vivid, and his spread thorough, but mistakes could still be made and he knew he was on the thinnest ice yet. But he appeared to pass the test. Connor gave his shoulder a firm squeeze, then left him to dispense encouragement amongst the men. Sean could be heard, tongue loosened by the liquor, loudly singing Dominic's praises. The big man affected shyness.

As the mood deepened, Connor and Seamus, and a couple of the others, vanished. When Seeler obliquely raised the subject of their disappearance with Sean, he was told they were in a private meeting. "Strictly by invitation only, bigfella. First division men."

But all eyes were on Dominic when Connor returned and invited him to join the meeting. As he followed Connor along the corridor, Seeler felt a nervous fluttering in his gut. Either he was being singled out for something important, or he was going to be the focus of intense suspicions.

He was led into a small dank room. The air was warm, wafting from a convector heater plugged into the mains. The air was rather thick with pungent cigarette smoke. Three whiskey bottles and a half dozen glasses, four of them containing liquor, stood on a rough table.

Connor closed the door. Three men stared at Seeler. Connor lifted an empty glass, filled it almost to the brim with whisky, then handed the glass to Seeler. "Health, Dominic."

Seeler nodded at the toast and took a satisfying swig. The spirit seared his throat. He felt it's warming progress down into his belly. "That's good. Aye."

Connor was speaking, introducing him to the others in the room, gesturing at each man as he spoke his name.

"Seamus you know. He's attached to the politicos. Feeds us their ideas, feeds them our frustrations, and hopes to make things meet in the middle. He's a long term member of the movement. He's done his share."

"Next, here's Matty." Seeler shook hands with a small, wiry individual, in his late forties. There was a calm about him, and his face was cheerful, at odds with the cicumstances of his work. "Matty is a master bomber. I know he won't mind if I say he's one of the most creative people we have. His successes have been far and wide. But his name and face are becoming known. We may have to send him away for a couple of years, let the Brits forget about him."

Matty's handshake was firm, his greeting brisk. "Glad to meet you, Dominic. Heard a lot of good things about you from the lads you trained in South Yemen. We'll be reuniting you with some of them in the next couple of days."

Connor moved on to the last man. A youth in his early twenties, with cropped hair, pale, gaunt face and small, weasel eyes that darted. He was thin, dressed in a tatty jumper, grimy jeans and heavy boots. His handshake was less than powerful, and as Seeler looked into his eyes he saw an eerie vacancy. The greeting this time was muted, barely a grunt, and Seeler had the sensation that he was looking the future of the movement. The old men, the veterans, for all their fervour, were real. They had character, weaknesses. They drank, loved women and married them, respected the church and sang the old songs when they drank. But the new breed had none of these characteristics. They were a strain reared in the hothouse of guerrilla warfare, born to the sound of the bomblast, the hailing of bullets, the bullying of the invading troops. They were a strain of cold, emotionless killers. He had heard the theories, now he had an inkling they were more than rumour.

"This is Ivan. He's also a master bomber. Conversant with virtually every new military technology that can be applied to our needs. He runs a bona fide armanents business in Manchester. This gets him invited to seminars and exhibitions by manufacturers. He is a respected dealer and exporter of weapons."

Seeler chipped in. "Doesn't that make him obvious; you know, coming from here and being openly involoved in the arms business?"

Connor's smile showed that he had been expecting that remark. "These are the new days, Dominic, how many times have we heard that? Ivan is here in Belfast for only the second time in his life."

When Seeler frowned, obviously wondering how someone who had not lived in Northern Ireland could be so involved in the IRA cause, Seamus chipped in.

"You remember how careful we had to be in the old days, Dominic? How the Special Branch used to find us? They would have a network of loose surveilance, loose, but enough of a net to be efficient. They could tell when something was up because our men would vanish from their homes. O'Shea the butcher and part-time bomber vanishes - the SB knows there's a bombing in the offing. Often the word would be spread on the mainland. Airports and dock security alerted to watch for individuals. Our boys would be picked up pretty quickly. These days, things are different." He refilled his glass, took a deep swallow, then continued, apparently unaffected. "We're learning. The smart move is to rear people on the mainland itself. From families steeped in the cause. Training takes place over there, and our people are encouraged to be normal. No extremism. Nothing to make them stand out. They can move without limitation, and properly trained can be more effective than anyone we can import."

Seeler nodded sagely, committing everything to memory. "So, why am I invited?"

Connor it was who answered. "Because in a way you are like Ivan. You've been away a long time, and you could probably be settled nicely. Ivan was set up in business by money from the cause. He has a good life."

"You see," Seamus chipped in."You have a degree of experience verging on the unique in this organisation. You've been around, seen and done a lot, and you are still effective. We want you to lead the team that hits London with the largest ever campaign."

*

Congreave and Burt wasted no time. The moment the van containing Seeler and the others had departed, they set about contacting Colonel Philips through the local army contingent. While they waited for the call back, they sat in their hotel room, drinking coffee and forcing themselves to make awkward conversation.

Jack asked Colin about the messenger they had met in the lobby. "His name is Seeler, and he's attached to the Covert Resources unit I was working for. He's renowned as the best all-rounder in the business."

"Why do you think he's over here?"

"I don't know. But you can bet your last pound the department would only send Seeler on an important mission. He's a very serious individual."

"What sort of mission?"

"Obviously an infiltration of an IRA active service unit. He must be in, and in deep, if he has access to Culum and Finnbar."

The telephone rang. Congreave snatched at the receiver, listened, then after a brief exchange, hung up.

"That was Philips. He'll see us. An army vehicle will be along to pick us up."

Philips listened gravely to their tale. "Incredible," he said when they had finished. "How all these things come together. You say he has the homing device working? Good, we'll organise a sweep. With any luck we'll be able to wrap up the whole group tonight." He pondered a moment, then asked what their plans were."

"We've decided to stay put and let them come." Burt told him. Philips frowned. "Gentlemen, let me recomend you stay here. This isn't the OK corral, you can't set a trap for these people. Civilians are likely to get hurt."

"I just want to get all this over with." Burt replied.

Philips looked wearied. The little conversation he had engaged in told him that Burt was stubborn and that his best hope in being listened to lay with Congreave, the professional. "Perhaps I didn't make myself clear. The two of you cannot go up against the IRA. You can't just walk in here, mop up a couple of hardened terrorists and be home in time for tea. Mr Congreave, you'd be doing your friend here a big favour if you explained to him just what the IRA is,and just what it is you are up against."

"I know exactly what I'm doing, Colonel." Burt cut back sharply. "But there are a couple of things you overlooked. Firstly, I'm not here to 'take on the IRA.' This is a personal matter. I'm here to get the justice the police would not give me. The fact that Strong and Craig are members of a terrorist group is incidental..."

"It is NOT incidental." Philips overrode him. "They are what they are because of the organisation they work in. The deaths of your family took place because of the IRA link. You can't expect the Provos to stand back while you eliminate two of their most able men."

Congreave could feel the heat being generated and decided to try and quell the flames. "Colonel, we're operating on the assumption that the killing took place without the sanction of the higher levels in the organisation. Even if the targetting had been correct, and it had been my family that died, it would still have been unlike the IRA to waste resources on a personal attack. I'm convinced the killings were the action of a renegade unit. I doubt the Brigade Chiefs even know the massacre happened. I'm equally convinced that once they do know, they'll do the politically correct thing and let us have them. "

Philips shook his head in resignation. He softly blew.

He was not getting anywhere. "You're crazy. You're going to get yourselves killed."

"This is personal," Burt insisted. "I don't give a damm about the poliitical arguments. The IRA fight is none of my business. Once this is over I'm on the next airplane to the states and I'm never setting foot in this part of the world again."

Congreave knew he had to alter the tack, get Philips on their side. He asked about Seeler, explained how he knew the big man, ending: "I don't want us messing up an operation. Just let us know where we can step safely."

Colonel Philips had, before coming to the meeting, checked out Congreave with Healey at Special Branch. He knew his high clearance was genuine, and knew he could be trusted. "It's strict need-to-know. But it's one of the big ones. We've never had a man in this deep before. Let me put it this way, he'd kill you before he'd let you blow things."

Burt stared at the SAS man with a degree of arrogance. "Don't forget, Colonel, I can take care of myself, and Colin here is a professional counter-terrorist. We'll be okay."

Philips stood, stared hard at Congreave. "I was giving you good advice, Colin. The smart move would be to get on the next flight out of here. But if you insist on staying, is there anything you need?"

"Weapons?" Colin chanced the question. Jack said quickly: "I for one would appreciate anything you could let us have."

Philips reined in the acidic remark that sprang to mind. He studied the man and knew he was a long way from trusting him. Looking once more to Congreave, he said:
"I'll see what I can do. Go back to your hotel and stay there. I'll have a few things sent over."
Congreave rose and shook the Colonel's hand. He thanked

Him, then followed Jack Burt's impatient figure from the room

*

Night deepened, the moon a silvery beacon that set the treetops shimmering. The Colonel piloted the surveilance vehicle along a deserted stretch of unlit country highway. Behind him a single soldier manned the console built into an equipment rack in the rear of the van. The Colonel had decided upon an impromptu look around to see if he could pick up Seeler's signal. Once he had, he could bring in a larger force and try for the entire active service unit at one swoop. For three hours he and the soldier had spelled each other, alternating between the steering wheel and the console where, on a circular VDU, an illuminated radius travelled clockwise, searching...

The soldier yawned and stretched out his arms. Hunched over the wheel, Colonel Philips called out: "Another five minutes and we'll swap."

"Yes Sir." At that moment a bleeping sound, faint but growing stronger, squeaked from the tiny loudspeaker in the console. The soldier's gaze sharpened as he focused on the glowing blip that appeared each time the radius swept over it. "Got it," he announced triumphantly.

Philips braked the vehicle and clambered into the rear. "Let's have a look at that map."

"Fragmentation, Dominic, that has been the saving of the movement. Spread thin but far, one cell not knowing what the others are doing, most of the time not even knowing who makes up the other cells."

"Must make it difficult to keep track of everyone. How does the chain of command hold together from Belfast?"

"It can be difficult. But we manage." Connor and Seeler were finishing off the whiskey, talking about the shipping of the Semtex and the weapons. They talked cache locations, and Seeler was given the names of the men he would be in control of once on the mainland. "They're a good group. You'll be making history, my friend."

Seeler smiled grimly. "Thank you for your confidence, Connor. I appreciate your taking me in so quickly. I feel less a stranger."

"We called you here, Dominic, and with good reason. A man of your experience is not something we find easily. Your work in Libya has benefitted the cause enormously. I believe you are on good terms with Qaddaffi himself."

"We've met." Seeler lied, aghast at how easily his infiltration had been completed. But unease gnawed at him. He knew that all good luck had to be paid for at some point. This was too good to last.

They joined the others, and an hour was spent telling each man his specific duties. Once every man knew what was expected of him, and the parcelling and shipping of the

Semtex and weapons was clear, Connor suggested they break for the night. "Tomorrow will be busy. Everything has to be loaded, and discreetly, and gotten onto the mainland. We'll be needing our wits about us."

No one argued. Perimeter patrols were detailed, and the first four men, armed with AK-47 automatic rifles, left to take up their posts. The rest retired to their rooms.

Seeler was billetted with Connor. As he sat on the edge of his bed, unlacing his boots, Connor kept up the conversation. Seeler asked if the perimeter guard was necessary. Connor stopped what he was doing. His face was grim. "Normally, perhaps not. This far south we're usually pretty safe. But I have a feeling, y'know."

Seeler did know. Making a mental note not to underestimate this man, who, for all his friendliness, would wipe him out in an instant if he for a moment suspected something, Seeler swung his feet into bed and pulled the drawstring that switched off the bulb overhead. In moments he was asleep.

Colonel Philips, having taken his bearings, decided upon an impromptu reconnaissance. Leaving the vehicle, he wended his way at a soft pace, keeping low, taking advantage of every scrap of cover, towards the farmhouse. The blackness of night had deepened. The moon ducking behind clouds and steeping the ground in a fathomless gloom that made Philips feel safe. Every few feet he stopped to listen, to divine the silence, but nothing stirred. The moon slid into view as clouds parted, and the house became starkly outlined, framed by a silvery rim, an old sprawling dwelling, surrounded by outhouses. There were five vans parked in shadow. The Colonel knew the number of vehicles was significant; groups of this size seldom met. Seeler was inside, and whatever was happening was of importance. The path was clear, nothing moved, and he felt the temptation to move in closer. As he crossed a clear patch of ground his confidence grew. Then he halted, heart in his mouth, when commanded to do so by a gruff Irish voice.

His mind worked fast - there might only be one man, but he would be armed. His senses probed the blackness in an attempt to locate his position. "I'm standing still," he said, raising his hands, hoping the man would speak again and so reveal his position. Mentally he rehearsed dropping to the ground and drawing his service weapon. He heard a soft crunch as the man took a step nearer, and Philips realised he was two metres away and slightly to the right.

The man took another step. He could now be seen in silhouette, an automatic rifle aimed from his hip. "What are you doing here, army, snooping?"

Philips tried to sound cheerful. "Just stopped for a pee, actually. I'm sorry if I've trespassed, I'll be happy to move on."

The man moved nearer. "I'll bet you would." His grip on the weapon shifted, and Philips knew the man was shaping up to club him. He prepared himself, and when the blow was swung he closed in with expert speed, nulling the attack before the man could complete the movement. He brought his knee up in a savage jerk that winded the Irishman, following up with a punch to the back of the neck. But before he could wrest the rifle from the Irishman's grip, a second gunman emerged from the blackness, crashing through the undergrowth. This man levelled his weapon and fired without hesitation, a single burst that took Philips in the thigh. He crumpled to the ground, hands clutched around the wound.

Rolling onto his back he looked up to see the second gunman standing over him, the tip of the rifle barrel inches from his chest. "Not another move, soldier boy." The man whispered. Verbal stealth was a habit with these men. "We have some talking to do, don't we?"

The shot had awakened the occupants of the house. Lights flashed on, voices cried out and the stone floored corridors echoed to the sounds of running feet. Seeler was deliberately cautious and did not rush out. Dressing, and ensuring that the gun in his possession was loaded, he walked the corridors, followed the sounds leading to the dank room where Murdoch had met his death. The noises resounded eerily. Excited raised voices. As the door came into view, and the voices became more distinct, a man cried out in pain and Seeler froze in his tracks, hand instinctively resting on the pistol in his waistband. It was Philips!

"You'll get nothing from me, you bastards. If you're smart you'll get your arses out of here. I'm not out here alone. My people will have heard the shot. You'll be surrounded before you know it."

Seeler made rapid calculations. What if Philips was bluffing? Finnbar would torture him, and the Colonel would break - everyone did sooner or later. He might even be forced to betray Seeler....

Could he take that chance with the assignment, and his own life? With the mission so close to being completed? He decided he could not. There was too much at stake. The bombing campaign had to be spoiled....

Swallowing hard, he took the gun from his waistband and held it at his side. He stepped resolutely into the room and paused just inside the doorway.

Philips was bound into the chair. He looked pale. His uniform was stained dark with blood. The fear on his face was starkly outlined by the rude glare from the bulb overhead.

He glanced up, saw Seeler, and their gazes met. Then Philips did the bravest thing Seeler had ever seen.

"My God," he gasped, a tremor in his voice. "Dominic McGarrigle. So you're back, you bastard. Have you the guts to do it this time?" His face was stretched taut in a convincing mask of defiance.

"Yes." Seeler replied blankly. And before anyone could react he took four steps into the room and put a bullet between Philips' eyes. His head kicked back, then slumped forward. His body sagged.

Seeler contained the turmoil raging inside of him. He calmly slotted the weapon back into his waistband.

A stunned calm had descended. The group members exchanged looks of amazement. Then Finnbar flared angrily. "Who the hell do you think you are?" He screeched. "You think you can take over? I'll show you!" He lunged.

Finnbar was tough and wiry, but Seeler was one of the most accomplished close-quarter combatants on earth. Deflecting Finn's punches with brisk ease, he sent him hurtling against a wall.

The others looked on in stupefaction. They looked to their leader for guidance. The four gunmen were twitching to act. Seeler was staring around. He knew he had to dominate here, had to make his mark with such force the others, hard as they were, would be intimidated. "Anybody else?" He noted the intrigued look on Connor's face. Then he was moving instinctively as one of the gunmen, in an attempt to impress his leaders, leapt at him. Seeler trapped the man's right arm between his own arms, and with a jerk snapped the arm at the elbow. The man fell to the ground, groaning. Seeler snatched the AK-47 and held it at his side. He waited, knowing this was the crucial moment. The room could erupt into violence at any instant.

"Calm everybody." It was Connor who spoke. His voice rang with authority. They all looked to him. "Do you want to tell us about this, Dominic?" He controlled his obvious anger well, and Seeler was glad of that for not even he could better the entire group if they attacked at once.

Finnbar forced himself to his feet. He was furious at having lost face. "You cost us dear. We could have gotten God-knows-what information from him!"

Seeler directed a contemptuous glare at him. "Wise up, Finnbar. Add it up; do you really think an SAS man of his rank would be out here alone? We're sitting here next to a thousand pounds of Semtex and any time now we're going to be surrounded by the army. We don't have time to chat, we have to get that stuff and ourselves out of here."

Finnbar was panting, so great was his fury, but he dare not attack again - the power in the big man's hands was phenomenal. Still, he could not stay quiet. "We could have taken him with us!"

"Sometimes you have to prioritise. I won't stand by and let you torture anyone else. To take a man's life is one thing, but you should always leave him something, some little shred of dignity. It's not necessary to reduce a man to a bleeding mess. I've no guts for your cowardly methods."

Finnbar was like a short leashed dog, desperate for attack but not sure he could get away with it. Connor interrupted. "There was something else in this case though, Dominic, something personal. Right?"

"There was. We clashed before and I made him a promise. Now all debts are paid."

Connor studied him for what seemed unending minutes. Dominic, the enigma. What strength, what power!

"Dominic is right." Culum spoke up. "There was no time for

anything else; we can't risk the campaign being soured. I vote we start loading the explosive."

Connor relented, but warned the big man: "You and I will talk later, Dominic. Let's move upstairs."

The explosives and cases of weapons and ammunition were fully loaded within forty minutes, and the men hurried indoors to busy themselves, industriously removing traces of their prescence. Outside the farmhouse Seamus, who was on point duty, impatiently paced the cobbled drive.

"Time's short. Everybody move out!" Connor called. He walked out through the front door and joined Seamus. "Are we still clear?"

Seamus, eyes shaded by his hand to eliminate the glare from the bright overhead moon, scanned the dark horizon. "So far...Wait!" he sucked in a breath. "Damm." His eyes narrowed as he peered harder. Headlights, perhaps a dozen sets, flitting through the dense patches of woodland that lined the lanes. "They're coming. I hope to Jesus we're not too late."

Connor raced back indoors to chivvy along the others. In moments the men were moving, filing briskly into the vans with a minimum of fuss. This was where they were good; obeying orders, moving quickly, going to ground. Engines roared and they were turning, in convoy, along the narrow lane that led east. Seeler, squatting in the rear of one of the vans, felt his pulse race. Beneath him the wheels throbbed dully and the whole vehicle swayed as they took tight corners at speed. Then someone cried out:

"Roadblock!" and a second voice hollered: "Hold on. I'm going through!" Seeler gritted his teeth, folded himself into a tighter ball and braced himself for the collision. A scream from the front sounded like Norm. Seeler pulled himself tighter. The van hurtled into the roadblock, forcing a wedge through the angled army vehicles, tearing metal, smashing glass. Seeler gripped an upright in the van and every bone in his body shuddered at the impact. For one horrible, yawing moment he thought the van would overturn, but it landed flat on it's wheels, bursting through like a bird winging free from a trap.

The engine roared in elation and the men packed claustrophobically tight around Seeler gave a rousing cheer, inspired more by adrenalin and the release of fear than by joy. Gunshots rang out as the soldiers fired at the speeding vehicles, then they were lost in the night and the van driver, who knew the warren of tiny lanes, proceeded to get them to safety.

Two hours later they drove onto a deserted industrial estate near the docks in Larne, north of Belfast. An empty warehouse was readied. Norm swung the van into it and braked quickly. The doors to the warehouse swung shut behind the van and the men tumbled out, blinking in the sudden glare as lights were snapped on.

Seeler looked around at his companions, saw the pinched faces of nervous men. He accepted a cigarette, and walked around the van as he puffed, inspecting the damage. The front was badly dented, great scorch marks gashed into the metal. And a web of cracks spread across one half of the windscreen where a bullet had cut through the glass.

Seamus had been in the first van to reach the warehouse. Now he approached the big man, greeted him.

"That was a close one. Are you alright?"

Seeler replied that he was, adding: "What now?"

Seamus glanced around the cavernous room. "There were five vans left the farm. We wait."

The men stood chatting in low, nervous voices. Seeler

saw Norm approaching, and they made stilted attempts at conversation. When Seeler moved, Norm remained close by. He sensed the big man was a survivor, and he wanted to survive too. He figured his own chances would be increased if he stayed in close proximity.

A horn sounded, the lights were dimmed and the vast doors opened silently. Another van roared into the warehouse, the engine being cut instantly. The moment the doors had closed a voice cried out for light and the huge overhead lamps were powered. The air was thick with exhaust fumes. A number of the men had coughing fits. The occupants of the van spilled out and the chatter became animated as they mingled with those already waiting. Sombody produced a couple of bottles of whiskey and the mood lightened.

Connor, Culum and Finnbar had been in the third van. Connor looked shaken as he and Seamus gathered the group around them.

"We lost the last van." He explained. There arose a murmuring as the men tried to gauge who was lost. Connor impatiently demanded quiet. "But the explosives and detonators and some of the weapons are intact. The army can't be far off our trail, so we prepare to move immediately for the docks. The container truck we are going to use is positioned behind this building. We take a short break while I divide us up into groups, then we start."

Seamus stepped forward. "Something else you have to know. The men we lost were to form the ASU heading the campaign in London. A few of you will have to accompany the shipment to the mainland to help get the stuff cached." He paused. "We'll come see you all individually about that. Take your break and be ready to move on the sayso."

Quickly the men were divided into three groups and given instructions. Seeler found himself grouped with Culum and

Finnbar. He joined these two in the rear of the van allocated them and squeezed into a tiny space. On impulse he glanced around, then said to Finnbar. "Where's Sean?"

Finn spat. "Bastard shit hisself and ran. The Brits shot him down like a dog. We're well rid of him, the coward."

Seeler paused to think. He could not help feeling sorry for the lad. He had hoped to talk to him, discover how he had gotten drawn into the organisation. The lad had both dreaded and yearned for action. Dreaded because he was naturally afraid, and yearned for because he desperately wanted to fit in. Seeler wished he'd kept an eye on him.

Someone handed him an SLR, a Sterling Light Rifle, probably taken from some dead British soldier, and a dozen ammunition clips. These he stored in his jacket, the rifle lay on his lap.

There was a flurry of prolonged activity as the Semtex, the boxes of detonators, and the few remaining weapons, rifles and ammunition, were secreted in the waiting container behind the warehouse. When everyone was ready, Connor sent away the two other groups. The container truck roared into life and the remaining van, containing the ringleaders, including Seeler, followed it. As he looked ahead, through the windscreen, Seeler saw the back of the container. He said, to no one in particular: "Anybody give a thought to what happens if that lot is hit?"

No one answered him.

*

25:

Along dark streets they ran at a steady pace, painfully conspicuous by travelling in convoy. The atmosphere in the van carrying the explosives was electric. Seamus was seated opposite Seeler. He broke the silence.

"Dominic, you don't mind helping us out by going with the stuff to the mainland?"

Seeler shrugged. "Here, there, it's all the same."

In the cab of the container truck Norm was sweating at the wheel. He had been in many tight spots, but there was something about driving a live bomb that scared the hell out of him. Beside him, Finnbar stared sullenly, his black gaze occassionally snagging on some passing object and following it out of sight.

Seated next to Seeler, Culum had his head between his raised knees. His dark curls bobbed as the van bounced. Seeler edged nearer, gave him a gentle nudge, and in a voice low enough not to be overheard said: "This messes up your plans, eh? More than likely Congreave and Burt will be gone when we get back."

Culum raised his head. Through the gloom the big man could see that his eyes were sad. "You know what, Dominic? I'm not really too bothered. There, I said it. And Finn wouldn't be too pleased to hear it, but what's done is done. Mary knew as well as anyone the risks we run. We had talked many times. She was willing to die for the cause, I know that. Congreave was just doing a job. As for Burt, it sounds as though he's suffered enough. If our paths don't cross I'll not be too upset."

Seeler asked him if he had ever killed anyone. "I have, Dominic. Oh yes I have. With the bomb mostly, though I once killed a man with a gun. Kneecappings used to sicken me, Finnbar's version especially, but I suppose if a man sees enough pain he can get used to anything."

Seeler shot a glance forward, at the container truck ahead. He was picturing Finnbar, drill in hand, closing in on the screaming Murdoch. Culum caught the look, and added: "Or even get to like anything, given the right motivation."

"Oh?" Seeler was glad to hear Culum talking. He wanted the man to open up, for once he had he would be easy meat when the killing time came.

"Dominic, don't judge Finnbar too harshly. You've seen hard times, I know that. You've seen death and it's ugliness." He hesitated, and his lips closed tightly, as if through habit; talking openly was not done. Weaknesses were not shown, despair not shared. Then drawing a full nasal breath, he took the plunge. "I've known dear Finn since we were kids. He had the sweetest nature..." he shook his head at some remembrance, then gulped, his look full of sorrow. "The Brits killed his family. His father had links with the organisation, but didn't want his kids to be involved. He wanted them to have a chance in life. The army burst into his house one night. There was a fracas, and his father was shot dead. His mother took the kids and drove off in a panic. She crashed the car. Only Finn survived. Twelve years old and alone in the world. The action, the shooting of his father, was blamed on our opposition, but it was the Brits alright. They do that sometimes y'know. Plant car bombs when things are too quiet, or when they want to invoke a surge of public support. They kill one of ours and blame the protestants. Kill one of theirs and blame us, or the INLA. They want us to kill each other off. It's a dirty war."

He stopped. Seeler, sensing the well was not yet dry, awaited more outpouring.

"All his family. Father, mother, younger brothers - two

of them. All gone. Within six months Finn was in the organisation as a runner and a messenger. He was a natural, all that bitterness and desperation, just the sort of recruit the organisation needed. By the time he was sixteen he had killed his first man. Now he's a fearsome creature. He feeds on hatred and fear."

Reaching the dockside enclosure, the container truck went ahead to be prepped for loading aboard a ferry leaving in two hours. The small group of men sat in the van, smoking. Seeler watched Connor walk across the parking lot to a flimsy wooden office where he shook hands with a man in an overlarge coat. After a brief exchange he returned to the van. Seeler's head was pillowed on his folded arms as he sat in the dark rear of the van. He dozed, only to be woken to the chill of the dawn by the sound of voices. In the cab, Finnbar and Culum, oblivious to his prescence, were arguing in fervent whispers.

"For Christ's sake, Finn. Just leave it will you?"

"No, Cully. No No No. Don't you see what a golden opportunity this is? Once I've called them they'll have no choice. It's brilliant!"

There followed a silence, during which Culum muttered something Seeler could not hear. Then Finnbar growled, and Seeler could picture the Irishman's face, distorted with hate as he turned upon his friend with piercing vehemence. "Well if you won't, Cully, I will. I'll not forget Mary. I'll make them pay!"

Furiously thrusting the door open he stormed out, slamming it shut again. The silence he left behind him was peculiarly heavy; the relief and the residue of fear leaving Culum's skin clammy. He crawled into the rear of the van and curled into a ball, as if hoping to doze.

"Trouble?" Seeler whispered. Culum started, like an

animal frightened in it's lair. He tensed to an attack position, relaxing only when 'Dominic' quickly identified himself.

Culum let out a massive sigh and crawled onto the wheel well. "No trouble. Just Finnbar degenerating into madness. Revenge at any cost."

Seeler digested this, guessing that Finn was planning another trap for Conreave and Burt. He said: "I hope you don't mind my saying I think Finnbar is a liability. He can't be easily controlled. He places his personal mission above his concerns for the cause. I'm surprised he's still in the organisation. I wouldn't tolerate him."

Culum was shaking his head. He knew the truth, but because of his lifelong friendship with Finn, he felt obliged to provide loyalty. "He's had a hard life. He's forgotten what it's like to be stable. For him, everything is a battle. Him against the world."

Seeler looked unconvinced. "He's a psychopathic killer hiding behind the cause. He's doing you no good."

As the silence extended, Culum seemed to withdraw within himself. To draw him out the big man asked if he was intending to move into a new safe house until the pressure from the army died down.

Culum looked at him in surprise, then realisation dawned on him. "Of course, you weren't outside when Connor was talking to us. He wants us to travel with Seamus and himself to replace the men he lost in the break from the farm. We're going with you to the mainland, to look after the explosives."

Seeler felt a chill creep slowly over him; things were slipping beyond control!

26:

Congreave emerged from the bathroom, rubbing at his hair with a thick towel. He was wearing an embroidered robe. Jack was on a stool before the mirror on the chest of drawers, running his buzzing electric shaver along his jawline. "Good morning." he called out.

Tossing down the towel, Colin sat on the bed and lifted the telephone from the bedside table and onto his lap. "I'll call Philips," he yelled above the noise from the shaver. "See how he got on." Trapping the receiver between neck and upraised shoulder, he dialled.

Putting the finishing touches to his shave, idly razing the stray whiskers he always seemed to miss, Jack watched Colin speaking into the receiver. When the expression on Colin's face dropped, Jack knew something was wrong and shut off the razor. "What is it?"

Colin slowly replaced the receiver. Although outwardly he appeared calm, Jack could see that he had paled.

"That was the adjutant at the Colonel's office. After our visit last night, Philips went out on a reconnaisance. He was taken prisoner by a group believed to be an IRA active service unit. By the time a squad arrived to get him out he was dead."

"Jeezus," Jack hissed. "That poor guy. Where the hell do WE go from here?"

27:

The sea was grey and choppy, with peaks that burst spectacularly against the hull of the ferry as it rolled ponderously, the vast bow dipping and rising as it dared the booming swell of the channel between Ireland and mainland Britain. The wind howled over the vessel, coming wet and fast, lashing every exposed surface with unremitting cruelty, patiently eroding and rusting.

At the barrier aft, Seeler leaned and stared over the expanse they had crossed. The thin strip of land had only moments earlier vanished beneath the horizon, and he became aware of the freighter's isolation. This feeling was intensified by the wind and the icy spray that dashed his face with numbing suddenness. His cheeks were stiff from the cold, and though he was cocooned in a borrowed thick overcoat, he was far from comfortable. Trails of water had permeated his clothing, and he wriggled from time to time in order to ease the niggling discomfort.

The exposed deck was not perhaps the ideal place to pass the journey, but he needed to think and this was the least inhabited spot on board. Drawing a hand from the depths of his coat pocket he massaged his numbed cheeks as he considered his moves. Once on the mainland he would have to act quickly if he wanted to reach the authorities and blow the bombing scheme. There would be no room for heroics, he could not take that chance, and once the group had dispersed it might prove impossible to unearth them later. They were good. They would go to ground with the survival instincts of the hunted animal and they would stay buried, until the time came to strike.

Seeler was good, but no one was that good. It was not

possible for him to destroy a cell of six hard men when each was a killer. He would have to reach a telephone, contact Healey at Special Branch, and get the locals moving.

His senses, that infallible warning system he had developed over many years, tingled warningly. He turned to see Connor and Seamus approaching unsteadily across the see-sawing deck. They were hauling themselves along the rail. His response to their greeting was suitably muted; he knew they had come to talk about his killing of Philips.

They joined him at the rail, one each side of him, then Connor spoke, his gaze not on Seeler but instead upon the churning waters below them, where a creamy foam trailed like excretia behind the freighter.

"Dominic..." he began, but the wind snatched away his voice. He turned his head, seemed to take a deep breath, and when he once more faced the wind he shouted. "Can't we go inside to talk?"

Receptive to any untoward movement from either man, Seeler turned his cold gaze upon Connor and further sensed the man's disquiet as the grey eyes bored into him.

"I'm comfortable here," Seeler replied. Then he smiled, and the incongruity of the smile in that cold place, that tense situation, sent a shiver along Connor's spine.

"Are you happy with the work we do, Dominic?"

"Do you doubt me?" The big man immediately cut back. Connor raised a hand in defence, then let it fall. "Your intentions, no. But your commitment....maybe. I have the distinct impression your heart is no longer in the cause."

"And what gave you that idea?"

"Your killing of the soldier. Your speech to Finnbar. We are not in the euthanasia business, we don't relieve people of their lives with dignity."

"That man's a fucking lunatic..." Seeler began. "If

being in the middle east taught me anything, it taught me not to work with amateurs. If you have to use them, you make sure they are kept at arm's length. Far enough away not to damage you. If he starts his psycho-tricks on the mainland he could get us all killed."

Connor smiled. "You started as a teenager. I seem to recall your record wasn't too different to his. Always in trouble; went abroad to avoid being killed."

"I was lucky. I learnt my lessons. I see the dangers and you can't blame me for not wanting to be killed because of a moron."

"He's wild, but he isn't stupid. When it comes to the cause I can trust him completely, and he'll take on jobs others want to avoid. In today's climate, men like him, the cold hearted, are the men we need." He paused. "If you've simply tired of the fight you can tell me - I won't judge you."

Seeler allowed an uncomfortable pause to develop. Then his mouth flexed into a rueful smile. "You're a shrewd gauger of men, Connor Black. Is it that obvious?"

"To most men, no. But I've been around this circuit before. Why did you come back? Was it the money? Were you short?"

"I thought maybe a change of scene would put fire back into my belly. I used to love a fight, used to love the sight of an army vehicle being hit by an RPG. I used to get all the kids going, throwing rocks at the army. I sent lads back here, well trained, and I'd see the newspapers, the results of my training, and I'd know they were my lads. The big ones; Harrods, the Hyde Park bandstand, the Baltic exchange."

"You did good work," Seamus chimed in. "You helped make the organisation what it is; the finest small army in the world. Through men like you we've made a laughing stock of the Brits' security."

Connor spoke again. His voice was serious. "We have four units on the mainland. There's no pressure. The Brits can't catch us. Our boys can stroll in or out at will. We were hoping you would form the core of the fifth unit, our first division team, if you like. Ready to go for the biggest one ever, then back home to safety."

"You have no worries, Dominic."Seamus said. "We're watertight. Think of it. The biggest one ever. A night of chaos the likes of which the Brits never dreamed of. We'll force the bastards out yet."

Seeler maintained his silence. He had not yet decided how to end things, but he knew events were drawing to a head. By the time the ferry docked, he had to have an action planned.

It was left to Connor to break the silence. "There's no shame attached to battle fatigue, Dominic. Once our business on the mainland is concluded, and Ivan has cached the Semtex your part is over. I'll get you a return ticket and you can leave with our blessing. From what I've heard of your exploits these past ten years you've earned at least that much." Despite the hard lines of his face, his expression had softened. He did understand. Seeler could not help liking the man for having the strength to show compassion.

Seeler thanked him, adding: "I'll think about what you said. If I'm not staying, what exactly do you want me to do?"

"We'll go over that later, about thirty minutes before we dock. Let's just say you have a vital part to play. There's not a man here with your experience. I'm sure you'll be a big help."

"Aye, like as not we'll be needing all your experience if we are to be shorthanded."

"What do you mean, shorthanded?"

"You know Seamus and I should never have been here. If we are taken an entire level of our organisation could be wiped out. But as you saw, our unit leaders were lost back in Belfast. Ivan can make the bombs, but he has to have support. You put it all in place for us, leaving me and Seamus to get home, and we'll owe you."

"Won't the others be enough? Culum and Finn and Norm, and the three others?"

"Culum and Finnbar have some personal business on the mainland. I don't know what it is and I didn't ask. But if Culum says it's important I'm inclined to give him the benefit of the doubt. To be honest with you..." Connor added quickly, with an airy wave of a hand. "When it comes to him running around on the mainland, I'd just as soon manage without Finnbar's peculiar talents."

"They'll be taking Norm Nunney with them of course," Seamus chipped in. "So you see, Dominic," he clapped Seeler on the shoulder. "You're in demand. I for one am glad to have you aboard."

Connor pushed himself away from the rail. "Will you come inside for a drink?"

Seeler, already sinking into thought, jerked himself back to full awareness and murmured that he would join them shortly. The Irishmen left him gladly for the warmth indoors.

He turned his face into the cutting spray, glad of the invigorating effect it had on him; he needed to be as awake as possible, and he wondered what business on the mainland could be vital enough to distract Culum and Finnbar from their course of revenge on Congreave and Burt.

28:

The ferry docked, and the laborious process of disembarkation began. The passengers, numbering over two hundred, gathered on the dockside and retrieved baggage as it came off a motorised trolley. Seven of the eight IRA men and Seeler separated, melting into the crowd. The container truck, driven by the eighth member of the group, was driven off and lined up with the other vehicles for customs clearance.

As he slowly made his way towards the immigration desk, Seeler frowned as he puzzled on how best to get the group members wrapped up. He disliked leaving this part of the process to chance, but events had been carrying him along in recent days. He was uncomfortable when he did not control the situation.

The papers he had been issued with by CORE were perfect, he knew there was virtually no chance of him being called aside for questioning. How then could he alert the authorities?

A wide smile flooded onto his face. Of course! How simple! The old sayings were true, the most obvious answer was usually the best. He had a pen. Carefully shielding his action with his body, he scribbled inside his passport then melted into the line once more. As he peered casually around he was dismayed to see Finnbar and Culum with Norm ahead of him in the line. The others, Connor and Seamus, with Ivan and the last man in the group, Kevin McGlory, were behind him. The burn of disatisfaction stung his throat. His mission had been to infiltrate and break up the cell, but it would have been a bonus to take out Finnbar. If he stayed to trap Connor and his men, the chances were that Finnbar and Culum would slip through.

As he watched, the three passed through the control area and made their way outside. Seeler contained his patience; he might get lucky - they might wait for him. Finn's old van might break down. Anything. Minutes later it was his turn to present his passport to the uniformed official behind the counter. He saw Connor, Seamus and the rest of the group strung out at intervals in the line tailing back to the entrance. The official flipped open the passport and Seeler felt a measure of satisfaction; he ought to at least halt the rest of the cell.

The official stared at the scribbled note in the passport for what seemed an interminable length of time. His face was calm, and Seeler was glad the man had sense enough not to react. At last, with a bored twist of his lips the official shut the passport and returned it. Seeler slid it inside his jacket and, with a sideways wink at Seamus, walked out through the exit.

A soft, damp morning breeze brushed his face. He took a deep breath. A rumbling in his gut reminded him he was hungry. Tyres squealed, and he caught sight of Finnbar's van as it sped across the parking lot and out through a gate.

"They're in a hurry," a voice said from behind him. He turned to see McGlory standing behind him. McGlory was thin, doughy faced, with a mousey moustache.

"Hmmm." Seeler responded. McGlory dropped the cigarette he had been smoking and ground it flat with his foot. "Yeah," he said. "Finn made a quick phone call, then he was itching to be off."

Seeler felt an odd tingling in his gut. The feeling that he had missed something. The van was some way off. He could see the top of it, speeding along, just visible beyond a high wall. He wondered...

When Jack entered the hotel room he found Colin seated on the bed, a shocked expression on his face. His white hands, clutching the telephone receiver, were on his lap. Jack felt a flush of fear; Colin looked like the worst thing in the world had just occurred.

Throwing down the newspapers he had been out to buy, Jack sank into a crouch before Colin and asked what was wrong. Colin looked at him, and there was a dreadful, haunted cast in his eyes. He was haggard and hollow cheeked. His eyes were dark orbs that burned intently.

"Colin, what the hell is wrong?"

Congreave took a breath. With a slow, deliberate motion he replaced the receiver. When he turned once more to face Jack, the American was chilled by the fear he saw.

"That was Finnbar Craig." Colin's words sounded unnaturally loud and clear. It was as if time, a moment in that room, had been frozen. Plucked aside and placed in isolation. "He's on the mainland. He sounded insane. He said he knew Anne and the kids are at PRISM. He said he..." His lips trembled. He was holding on for all he was worth. "He knows they are there. He's on his way there now to....pay me back for Mary." His voice quivered and his eyes brimmed with tears as he hovered at breaking point. He swallowed a lump so hard he had to force it down.

"He dared me to meet him there. He said he'd give me a fighting chance to save them. Jack, what am I going to do?"

Jack moved to Congreave's side. He gave his arm a squeeze. "You're gonna go meet him, pal. We both are. And we're going to wipe the son of a bitch off the face of the earth."

The corners of Congreave's mouth arched downwards as he face was stretched into a mask of wretchedness. He squeezed tight every muscle in an attempt to lock down the fear. "You don't understand. He's on the mainland. We can't get there in time. He'll never let them live..." His mouth fell open, his eyes opened wide. "Oh God, what have I done?"

Jack leapt to the telephone and pressed for a line. Digging into his pocket for a diary, he thumbed the pages, found the emergency number at PRISM. "I'll talk to Parsons," he said, sure that Congreave was not hearing him. "He'll get your family to safety. Just hang on."

Parsons took the call, and as he listened he felt a familiar chill seep over him - a sensation he had not experienced since his days at CORE, the cold knowledge of impending and unavoidable deadly conflict. Clearing his throat, he summoned Sam Ellis by intercom and told him what was happening.

"What do you want me to do?" Sam asked.

"Clear the place, Sam. Everybody out. Get Anne and the youngsters up to the cottage."

Reading something in his friend's tone, Sam asked: "We're going too, aren't we David?"

Parsons could not meet his stare. Sam pressed him. "David?"

"You go Sam. I have an investment to protect here."

Sam stared at him with disbelief. "Are you mad? What do you mean, investment? You have insurance don't you? You're not thinking of facing these people?"

Parsons smiled. "Sam, they have no quarrel with me. Once they see I'm alone here they'll move on. And if they get rough, don't forget I've faced worse than these - and lived."

"You were younger then, David. You've been out too long. We both have."

Parsons stared at his desk blotter in stubborn silence. Sam teetered on the brink of further argument, then relented. He knew better than to try and deflect David Parsons once his mind was made up.

Parsons glanced up, saw Sam's frustration and rewarded his friend with a half hearted smile. "Look, you know Colin's an old friend. I have to be on hand to help if I can. You would do the same, and don't try to tell me you wouldn't. Believe me, I won't be running any risks."

"Go on Sam, get them up to the cottage. I don't know how long we've got."

Jack Burt carried a tumbler of water from the bathroom and handed it to Colin. The glass sat unnoticed in his hand. He continued to stare as though in shock.

Jack squatted before him. "Colin, pull yourself together. Parsons assured me he will get Anne and the kids to safety. Come on now, I need you .You have to tell me what to do next; who do we call to get a flight out of here? What strings can we pull?"

"I'm gone, Jack. I shouldn't have killed Mary Morrison. I could have taken her alive. I brought disaster to you, and now my actions will hurt other innocent people."

"C'mon," the American chivvied him. "That's no way to talk. We can do this."

"I shouldn't have killed her..."

"If you hadn't, she'd have gone free. She'd have gotten off. She would be out there now, planting bombs. Killing people. Come on. We have to get moving."

Colin's eyes were still wide. Terror lurked behind them. "I can't go Jack. If what happened to your family were to happen to mine I couldn't take it. Going in with me will be a risk. I'd be worrying. Be easy meat. I wouldn't save them and I'd probably get you killed too."

"Hell," Jack growled. "If you do nothing your family will die. I want those bastards, and I've nothing to lose. So don't you go worrying about me. Come on, let's get moving."

Colin shook his head, kept on shaking it. "No, no I can't."

Anger spumed quickly within the American. A surge he did not want to hold down. "Damm you," he muttered, rising to his feet. "Get up and fight!" When this elicited no response he snatched the tumbler from Colin's grasp and hurled the water onto his face. "GET UP! Don't crap out on us now, Congreave. Anne needs you. The kids need you. Get off your ass and *do* something!"

Colin sat dumbly, water trailing down his face, dripping from the ends of his hair, coursing down his face. He started to inhale deeply, gathering himself. Then he dry swallowed, and in a voice charged with released energy, said:

"Get me a towel. I'll make the calls."

*

30:

Police cars descended on the dockside in a haze of sirens and flashing blue lights. Most of the Irish group had been delayed indoors. Those who were in the parking lot were easily mopped up. Weaponless, even Connor and Seamus were easily taken. They cursed loudly, suspicions roused, and Seeler joined in, playing the role to the end.

"What do I do, Connor?" he called out as police officers poured out of cars and vans, weapons cocked.

"Say nothing, Dominic. Say nothing. Someone will be in touch" Connor's words were choked off as he was forced onto the bonnet of a car, his hands pulled behind him and his wrists cuffed. "Don't give the bastards any chance.!"

Seeler was cuffed, thrown into the rear of a police car. He noticed that every one of the group was placed into a separate vehicle. This measure, he realised, was taken to protect him in case there proved a further need of his cover. Silently he gave thanks for the man with the organisational foresight to think of the move.

He found himself seated next to an important looking officer in the rear of the car. "You're Seeler?" the officer asked as the car moved forward. He extended a hand. "Bainbridge, anti-terrorist squad. That was good work." Seeler thanked him, adding: "You were pretty quick off the mark yourself. Forty minutes was better than I expected."

"We had a drill last month. We're still pretty hot. Tell me, what's the history of the group. Who have we nabbed?"

As they journeyed Seeler poured out information. Bainbridge was fulsome in his praise. One might have thought Seeler had conveniently arranged for the terrorists to walk blindly into police custody.

As the car sped along a stretch of motorway, following the

others in convoy, Seeler recounted his experiences. The words flooded from him in an organised, cathartic fashion; the result of too much time spent under pressure. He reeled off names and locations he remembered, carefully omitting his killing of Colonel Philips. On this point he knew he had overstepped the mark; he had made many enemies over the years, people who feared him. Who would leap at the chance to put him down. The knowledge he had killed a British soldier would give them powerful leverage. Even so, he was vulnerable; if one of the other cell members opened up, told of Dominic's murder of the dreaded Brit, perhaps trying to cut a deal for a lighter sentence, who knew what pressures would be brought to bear on Seeler?

Bainbridge listened, nodding as he took mental note. He said: "Healey and I have spoken on a number of occasions. I called him when the message came in and he gave me some background on you. I'm impressed."

"The three who slipped through were Culum Strong, Norm Nunny and Finnbar Craig. I should be able to give you detailed descriptions. I don't know where they were heading, but the van ought to be fairly easy to spot." He described the vehicle. Bainbridge had the officer next to the driver radio an alert for the van, then he sat back and offered Seeler a cigarette.

"Relax," he said. "It's all over bar the shouting."

*

Jack spent a couple of hours on the telephone trying to hire a small aircraft, but to no avail. No matter how much money he wanted to spend, there was not a private aircraft for hire. Finally Congreave made a telephone call, to Michael Collins, the Director at Covert Resources in British Intelligence. A promise was made, and after an hour spent restlessly pacing the floor of the hotel room, the return call came. Congreave shook a fist in triumph as Collins gave him the news he wanted. He hung up and grabbed his coat. "Come on," he said excitedly.

Jack was already primed. "He's done it? Where do we go?"

Congreave was scribbling on a scrap of paper, committing details to paper while still fresh in his mind. "Let's go get that car."

They had hired a car earlier, knowing they would have to drive to whatever field the aircraft would leave from. They rushed down to the lobby, settled the bill and left.

Jack hurled the bags in the rear of the car while Colin spoke to the porter, trying to learn the quickest route to the airfield. He hurried out, climbed into the driving seat and gunned the engine.

"You know where we're going?" Jack asked. Colin nodded. "I think so." He swung the wheel savagely, cutting a swathe through the busy flow of traffic. Horns sounded in angry chorus. Jack scowled, hating being a passenger. "Take it easy," he growled as Colin narrowly avoided hitting a truck. "You'll get us killed."

"Fuck that. We have to get to that field."

He thumped the horn, and his face contorted with rage as he spun the wheel again.

Within two hours they were airborne. The midday sun was high in a near cloudless sky, and the grey expanse of the Irish channel glistened far below them. The aircraft, a tiny Cessna, roared lustily, the sound loud enough to rendered any attempt at conversation useless.

Congreave and Jack sat in brooding silence. Each buried amongst his own thoughts. Jack was dwelling on the past, thinking about Carol. How he missed her, the smell of her hair, the warmth of her. Her kiss. He felt a lump growing in his throat. A tear swelled at the corner of an eye. The kids, the kids.....

Colin's mind was focused on one thing; family. Anne. The kids. He was making a concerted effort not to dwell on the difficulties. Unease gnawed at him, for he was convinced he was going to lose them. Sure it was all going to go disastrously wrong. And then there was the fear. A fear so strong. Like nothing he had ever felt before. He had been afraid before - of course he had. But it had never been this intense. Not just his life on the line this time. Anne. The kids.

The two men exchanged looks. Ahead, they both knew, lay a bitter battle - and death for somebody.

Reaching out, Colin gave Jack's arm a squeeze of encouragement. "Stay angry, but don't let it get away from you. You have to use the anger. That's the secret."

Jack nodded dumbly. He knew that. He was ready.

The airstrip nearest PRISM was still over one hundred miles away from the camp. As the small aircraft made it's approach Colin's nervousness increased. The tension in the Cessna had continued to wind tighter until the two men felt like snapping and lashing out. Colin had started to gnaw, unconsciously, at the white knuckles of a clenched fist. "Will you stop that?" Jack complained. "You're making me nervous."

"I just hope to Christ there's a car to be had when we land." Congreave said, ignoring Jack's protest. "We're running out of time."

Seeing the strain his friend was under, and realising with a twinge of confused guilt that he now considered Congreave a friend, Jack gave a pale, slightly rueful smile, and attempted to calm him with reasoning. "They have a four hour lead - tops. We know that last night they were with Seeler at the hotel, and the earliest they could have sailed was six o'clock. There were no very early flights, and it's unlikely they would fly in the knowledge that security would be tight after the killing of Philips. So they probably sailed. And if they did sail, their lead is cut to nothing. We'll get there first."

Congreave shook his head. "I'm not so sure. I have a bad feeling about this."

"Trust me, Colin. Parsons has them safe."

"We don't know that!" Colin almost exploded with the pressure.

"We do know that." Jack was surprised with his own control. "Stop worrying."

The aircraft lurched suddenly, and both men clutched at hanging straps to steady themselves. The little craft touched the airstrip with a heavy bounce and a squeal as the rubber tyres scorched the tarmac. They taxied to the nearest bay, cleared the formalities as quickly as possible, then dashed into the small control building and asked to use the telephone. There was no hire car facility at what was little more than a private field. They called the nearest town and ordered a cab. More frustrating minutes were expended, and when the car arrived, they harried the driver to hurry back into town, to the nearest hire office. At last it seemed their luck was changing.

The hire of the car went smoothly. Filling the tank, they set off for the camp at breakneck speed, and after taking wrong turns and being forced to double back upon themselves, they at last reached a stretch of road Congreave recognised as being close to PRISM. He had raged at the wheel, and Jack, equally anxious, held back the acid remarks that sprang to mind, reminding himself that, professional though he was, Colin was still human, and he was almost crazed with anxiety.

They arrived in the valley as dusk began to bathe the hillsides with mottled gold. The lights in the camp far below twinkled promisingly.

"Looks normal enough." Jack said, breathing a sigh of relief. He had exchanged places with Colin and now he pressed upon the accelerator, sending the car down the slope that led to the camp.

"Cut the engine, and the lights." Colin instructed when they were a mile from the camp. "If they are here we don't want to give too much away."

"If they're here," Jack remarked dryly. "They'll have seen the lights by now." The car coasted in darkness to a halt by the roadside.

"Wish we had a weapon." Jack muttered. Colin murmured agreement. In Belfast, Colonel Philips had implied he would help arm them, but once he was gone they were left alone. They would have to walk into the camp, face whatever waited them inside, unarmed.

"We'll be careful. We'll be okay." Colin whispered. His tone had become flat and dull, and Jack, witnessing the startling metamorphosis his friend had undergone during the final miles, felt a fresh surge of confidence. Colin had reverted to operational type; instinctively begun to prepare himself. Jack was reminded of that night in the taunt him.

"How do you know?"

"Jungle sense." Jack said. "'bout the only useful thing I brought back from Vietnam. I forgot I had it until just now." He glanced around as though drawing something from the air. "They've been here, but they're not here now."

Still cautious they began to explore the buildings one by one. The interiors appeared undisturbed. The occupants had packed and gone. "Weird, isn't it?" Jack muttered. "Signs of life everywhere but nothing moving."

The cottage where the Congreaves had been staying was the only building to show signs of being vacated hastily. Wardrobe doors gaped open to reveal desolate interiors. Inside of them, tangled wire hangers created weird skeletal forms. Fresh flowers still shone, spilling from vases in vivid splashes. Dishes were stacked, unwashed, on the drainer.

Colin at last allowed himself a sigh of relief. His greatest fear had not been realised. "Well at least they seem to have gotten away." He glanced at Jack, saw the good humoured grimace that divided his face, and could not help smiling himself. "Okay, you told me so."

Jack clapped him on the shoulder. "Let's finish searching this son-of-a-gun, shall we?"

At last there remained only the gymnasium. As they stepped into the short corridor that separated the changing rooms from the gym, Jack put out a hand to stall Colin. "Slow down," he whispered. In reply to Colin's inquiring look, he whispered: "Just a feeling."

Nerves stretched, they moved along the corridor at a crawl. Colin was first to peek through the small square window in the gym door. He let out a gasp, "Oh Jesus!" and burst in, Jack following.

Slowly they approached the centre of the room where a thick supporting pillar thrust upward, fanning out at the apex to take the weight of the domed, glass ceiling.

David Parsons was bound to the pillar. A length of bloodied rope, drawn across his eyes and knotted tightly behind the pillar, held up his head. Darkening trails of drying blood scarred his pale cheeks. The smooth floor around his bare feet, around his crushed and scarlet toes, was speckled with red.

"Oh my God," Colin muttered weakly as he stood before his friend's tortured body. His gaze ran from head to foot, taking in the horrific injuries. Parsons' shirt was open, exposing his chest. A bloody letter M had been carved into white flesh.

And his throat had been cut.

Jack felt revulsion stir within him and he thought at first that he would vomit. Taking deep breaths he was able to stay level, but the feeling did not diminish, it coalesced into a white hot fury. "They have to pay." He heard himself saying in a voice he scarcely recognised as his own. It was hard. Startling. Even Colin, caught up in his own anger, looked at him in surprise.

"The bastards." Colin muttered. A tear formed in the corner of one eye and he wiped it away.

Jack raised a finger to his lips as the sound of footsteps sounded in the corridor. Acting upon some unspoken signal the two men moved to positions at opposite sides of the room and took cover behind pieces of apparatus.

Sam Ellis burst into the gymnasium. His shocked gaze fell upon Parsons, and a broken cry burst from him: "David!" He fell to his knees. He was not a man who cried easily, but a great sob shook his body. A tormented groan wrung from deep within him as he covered his face with his hands.

Congreave and Burt emerged from their cover and walked towards him. He did not hear them approach, and as they helped him to his feet and led him from the room he did not question their prescence. He shuffled between them, staring in stupefaction at the floor.

They carried Sam into the canteen. Sandwiches lay in the trays on the counter and the coffee in the cona was still hot. Grouped around a table the three ate and drank without tasting. Jack and Colin exchanging grave glances. Sam shakily accepted a cigarette. He puffed on it feverishly, his eyes haunted.

Slowly, painfully, he began to talk. "I knew you'd come." He stumbled out. "All the way back here I knew there'd be bad news waiting...and I knew you'd be here."

"Back from where, Sam?" Jack probed."Where did you go?"

"What happened to my family?" Colin asked, his anxieties renewed after finding Parsons.

Sam told them he had taken Anne and the children to a cottage he and Parsons maintained for emergencies in the mountains. "Occasionally we get a group stranded out there in the hills. There's warmth and plenty of food. They'll be fine."

"What I don't understand is why they left here so quickly." Jack said. "They must have known we'd come here, so why leave? It can't be they're scared of us."

An uncomfortable idea had crystalised in Colin's mind. He felt uneasy dwelling on it, but said: "Is there any chance they could find this cottage?"

Sam ground his cigarette stub flat in the ashtray. "It's unlikely. All the trainees who might have known about it have gone. Apart from them, only David and I knew...."

"Shit," Jack cut in."They tortured him for Christ's

sake." He looked to Colin. "Do you think he talked?" Colin was frowning. Eyes unblinking. "Anybody would talk under that kind of pressure." An icy weight had settled in his gut. He knew.

He knew.

Sam, still numbed by grief, was last to realise. "But if he told them, that explains why they left..."

As one, the three men rose.

Led by Sam they went directly to a locker room filled with cabinets containing weapons, heavy jackets, and a multitude of outdoor equipment. Sam, overriding the protests of the other two insisted on kitting them out fully before setting off.

"Listen, the hills are tough. The weather can be a bitch and there's no way to get there but on foot. And if you lose me, touch wood, you could be lost out there. We go prepared or we don't go at all."

Sam flipped open a large map book onto an oak table and briskly marked the location of the cottage with his thumb. "This is the spot. As you can see, it is remote. I doubt they'd find it without pretty specific directions. I don't believe David would give them what they wanted."

Colin still looked uneasy. "Dave was like a brother to me, Sam, but the fact is they've gone. We have to be prepared for the worst."

Jack lifted an automatic pistol from one of the lockers and hefted the weight. "Let's stop jerking around, Sam, let's go."

The grief Sam had controlled so well in the minutes since leaving the canteen, now welled up on a wave of frustration and his anger at the impatience of the others broke free: "For Christ's sake. These men are vicious killers! If you want to survive you are going to need every ounce of edge you can get. So stop squabbling and shape up!" The scottish burr of his accent became pronounced with his anger, his words brimming over into each other.

The two remained silent while Sam pulled equipment from the lockers; heavy jackets for warmth, rucksacks containing emergency ration packs. Weapons. He gave each of them a Browning Hi-power pistol and spare magazines of ammunition. To Jack he said:"Check that. Are you comfortable with it?"

Jack said he was. Sam repeated his question, this time to Colin. Congreave was already checking the weapon. He rammed a magazine into the handle, and checked the action. It was obvious he was at home with a gun, and Jack permitted himself a grim smile; Finnbar and his friends were in for one hell of a tussle!

As they prepared to leave, Colin, acting on some unexplainable impulse, glanced into one of the other offices. On the desk he found a map, opened flat. A location had been circled in red felt tip, a glaring circle. He called to Sam and received the confirmation of his darkest fear.The circle location was the cottage. He felt his heart sink.

When they were kitted out to his satisfaction, in heavy boots and warm clothes, and loaded with essentials in backpacks, Sam led them out. Towards hills so tall the tops were lost in the night.

*

31:

Moonlight played on the slopes; a patch of silver here, a bottomless black hollow there. Floodlighting in stark relief the path ahead.

Talking was kept to the minimum on Sam's orders. The slightest sound, he warned, could be carried for miles if the wind favoured it. Looking relaxed and completely at ease in this environment he led the way. Night made no difference, these were his hills.

Trudging behind Sam, Jack soon became aware of the layer of perspiration that coated him inside his thick clothing. The air was cool, but the exertion of backpacking and the mounting excitement set his pores to work. He wondered whether Colin, plodding silently behind him, was experiencing the same thing.

Colin was not. His field of concentration had narrowed to shut out all distractions; a skill he had honed over the years spent in covert operations, where survival was a direct result of preparation and focus. He was on the most serious mission of his career and there must be no mistakes. He felt no fatigue. Just kept his gaze on the path ahead, intent on covering ground.

Three hours after setting out, Sam waved them to a halt. They settled gratefully onto the cool, mossy earth. Unearthing a flask and cups from his pack, Sam handed out hot coffee.

Colin had been reluctant to stop, but was surprised at how relieved he was once he did. His entire body ached. The coffee was swallowed and he asked Sam how much further it was to the cottage.

"Another hour or so." was the reply. Sam had his hands cupped around a cigarette in his mouth. He sucked on it gratefully. "God, that's good."

Jack chuckled. "You old hypocrite. Preaching healthy living to us when all the time you're puffing your life away."

"Hey," Sam joked, his voice gravelly. "Remember I'm not paying to get fit. Besides, old habits...you know."

Jack nodded. Colin broke in, his voice grave. "Sam, this cottage. What's the terrain? How do we make our approach?"

"Straight ahead. That's the simplest way. But I'll go in alone while the two of you cover me." Colin started to protest, but Sam shut him down. "We don't want to walk into a trap, do we? They could be in there, waiting."

"He's right." Jack chipped in. "This way, if Sam is taken prisoner we'll still have the opportunity to get him and your family out with the knowledge of what we're up against."

Colin grudgingly conceded it would be pointless to commit all three of them to the unknown. He was silent while Sam outlined his scheme. "Once in, I'll signal. There are walkie-talkies in the packs. If by some chance the irishmen are in there, they'll probably try to force me to lure you in. In that event I'll say the words 'All clear.' If you hear that, the rest is up to you, though I'll do whatever I can from the inside. If I tell you that everything is fine, you'll know I have Anne and the kids safe. I'll bring them out to you. You stay outside, understand? We can't risk us all being caught indoors."

The others nodded. Sam drained his cup, tipped out the dregs, then screwed the cap back onto the flask. He eased himself to his feet. "Let's be off then. Another hour should do it."

When they were on their feet, Colin put a hand and grasped Sam's arm. "I appreciate all you're doing, Sam. This isn't your fight."

Sam's reply chilled him. "This became my fight when those bastards killed David. I'm going to see them all dead."

They made good time, arriving on the edge of the plain where the cottage stood almost exactly one hour later. The solid black shape of the building was outlined with sinister clarity against the greying sky.

"Be dawn before we know it." Jack muttered. At a command from Sam, he and Colin dropped to the ground. "You're clear on what to do?" he hissed.

"Get on with it!" Colin snapped. Sam bit down the stinging rebuke that leapt to mind, reminding himself that the man was worried sick about his family. He sprang to his feet with the energy of a much younger man and moved away. The other two watched his figure shrink as it neared the cottage.

"Do you think they are already there?" Jack asked. Colin shrugged. "It's possible. Or they might've gotten lost. It could even be that Dave Parsons gave them the wrong route to buy us more time."

"He'd have to be one hell of a strong man to do that."

"He was." Colin meant to say more, but the walkie-talkie crackled into life, startling him.

"Sam here. Everything is fine, repeat, everything is fine. Colin, I have someone here who wants to talk to you." A second voice burst from the set. It was tinny, but unmistakable; Anne. "Colin, Colin, we're okay. I'm glad you're here!"

He breathed a sigh of relief, then lifted the handset to his lips. "Good to hear you too, love. Are the kids alright?"

"They're sleeping."

"Okay. Honey, get your things. Sam will bring you all out. I'll be waiting here."

"Will do. Over and out..." he heard her giggle just before the transmission was cut.

The tension in the atmosphere had lessened. Jack shook Colin's hand. His grip was firm, but when he spoke there was a catch in his voice. "I'm glad for you, buddy. Really glad."

The two men relaxed a little. Colin slipped off his pack and stood to stretch. His gaze idly traversed the horizon, then he stiffened. Three or four dark figures had appeared in the distance, outlined against the lightening sky. He felt fear clutch at him. "Jack..."

Burt registered the change in Colin's tone and was instantly alert. He sprang to his feet, and, shielding his eyes with his hand, he peered across the dark expanse. "I see them. Jeez, do we need this?"

Instead of answering, Colin began to mutter urgently into his walkie-talkie. "Sam! Sam, they're here!"

"What?" Sam's voice squawked back at him. "Where?"

"Coming in from the left of our position. Three or four of them. Maybe half a mile away. They've seen the cottage."

"What do you want me to do?"

"Bring them out - and fast. But stay low. If they see you they might get excited and start shooting. If that happens keep going. Jack and I will intercept. Now go!"

"Roger."

Jack was already squaring the pack on his shoulders. "We can't run," he said. "We'd be too conspicuous. We have to go in low."

Colin rummaged in his pack and produced two weapons. Handing one to Jack with a curt, "Follow me," he began to follow a zigzagging path at a low, crouching run. The small group was plainly visible on the horizon. They were three hundred metres from the cottage and making for it heedless of any trap that might await them. They did not look around. Obviously they believed they were safe. Colin, deciding to exploit their lack of awareness to the full, hared towards them at breakneck speed. His heart pounded. His mind focusing laser-like on the group he now saw numbered three. He was drawing close enough to almost pick out details. Light was coming on quickly. A luminous ceiling of massed white cloud approached over the horizon.

"Colin!" Jack risked a loud whisper. He was panting as he struggled to keep up. "Slow down!" He shot a glance towards the cottage and saw a small huddle, two large and two small figures, hastening away from the building. He felt relief wash over him. "Way to go, Sam."

From ahead came a shout. Colin had been spotted. A shot rang out and Jack, on instinct, dived for the ground and rolled over and over on the moss. When he came to a halt, gun grasped firmly in his outstretched hands, and peered ahead, there was nothing to be seen. The horizon was uncluttered. The killers had gone to ground.

There came a burst from the walkie-talkies as Sam and Colin exchanged signals. "Well done, Sam. Now get them out of here."

"Be back for you later. Over."

Jack shinnied along the ground on his elbows until he was alongside Congreave. The Englishman grinned at him, his thin face taut and skull-like in the feeble light.

"No ducking out now, Jack."

Jack swallowed dryly, but managed a smile. "It's showtime."

Colin tensed, pressed his face to the earth, as a shadowy figure appeared above the horizon and loosed a short burst of gunfire. The shots struck the ground thirty metres away, sending clods of earth flying. Then the figure vanished as rapidly as it appeared.

"They don't know exactly where we are. That was a shot in the dark."

Jack winced at the pun, adding: "It wasn't that far out."

"Be ready." Colin warned. "They'll be up for another crack anytime now." Almost before he had finished speaking, a black figure reared over the hillock and swung a weapon. Colin fired, three rapid shots, and the figure fell back. A cry rang out, unnervingly clear in the still air. "Cully! Finnbar! I'm hit!"

There came the sound of voices, then a wild cry electrified the atmosphere. "Come on Congreave! We're ready for you. Remember Mary?" The voice rose to screeching pitch. "You're gonna pay. Run, while you can!"

Jack looked at Colin to see his reaction, but the Englishman appeared unmoved. His gaze raked the ground ahead, and his hand held the gun ready. "What now?" He asked him.

"We wait," Congreave replied.

The walkie talkie crackled. "Colin, are you still receiving me?" Colin responded. "What is it, Sam?"

"We're virtually clear. Give me a few hours and I'll be back for you. Over."

"That's going to be dangerous, Sam."

"But if I don't do it how will you get back?"

"Good thinking." Colin chuckled. "Be careful. Over."

"Try to stay within range of the cottage. That'll make it easier to find you. Over."

"Understood. Thanks Sam. Once again, be careful."

"Oh I will. Never fear."

On Colin's signal, Jack followed him along the slope, working a path intended to take them around the hillock where the Irishmen had concealed themselves.

"They'll be moving." Jack said, urging for more speed. Colin agreed, but, arguing caution, added:"We can't take the chance they haven't."

At last they stood poised, some two hundred metres east of the hillock and ready to take the crest to view the other side. On Congreave's signal they ran in, keeping low, guns ready, eyes keening for any movement ahead. Then he halted, held up his hand. Jack braked beside him.

"They've moved....look." Jack stared where directed. The oncoming daylight, though still pale, was sufficient to enable them to see the undisturbed plain ahead. "Where did they go?"

Colin jabbed a finger towards the east, where a dark sea of trees filled the expanse between two massive, shale sided mountains. "The forest," Colin muttered. "The only decent cover for miles. That's where they'll be."

Jack chewed absently on his lower lip. "We could probably get away from here."

"I know, but then I'd spend the rest of my life looking over my shoulder. This has to end."

Jack sighed. "Well, if you insist on going in, I'm here to do it with you, pal. You want to lead the way?"

"Maybe you ought to lead the way. You at least had experience of fighting in Vietnam."

"That was twenty years ago." Jack remonstrated. Then his voice changed. "Are you trying to tell me something?"

"Just that I've specialised in working alone. Killing people at close range. Sniping from buildings, planting bombs. Jungle warfare is something I've never had the pleasure of."

Jack shook his head. "Well that's filled me with confidence. I should've made you do Parsons' course." he fidgetted to square the backpack. "Okay, stay alert and follow me."

32:

A convoy of police vehicles, over a dozen vans and cars with a motorcycle escort, headed south along the M6, powering past the already fast traffic. Into the capital they poured, crossing the river into Rotherhithe, and arriving at the high security compound, The Cellars. The members of the Irish group were kept separate through processing and led to individual cells. Interrogators, specialists, arrived in elated mood. They had a prime catch to work with.

Seeler was driven straight to Century House where he met up with Michael Collins, the Director of CORE, who walked with him to the debriefing room. "How was it?" he asked.

"It was no picnic." Seeler replied. He was still feeling tense. He rubbed at the side of his neck where his shirt collar chafed. "I'll be glad to get out of these clothes. I've been in them for two weeks."

"Healy's running the interrogations down at the The Cellars. They may want you to show your face later, to further entrench your cover, so don't throw out your gear or shave. It might be better if you don't wash your hair."

Seeler winced. "Do you mind if I brush my teeth?"

Collins, smiling, thought for a moment, then said, yes, he might allow it.

In the cramped briefing room, sitting alongside Collins and two dull suited male assistants, there to report back to their respective department heads, Seeler told his tale. After a lengthy question and answer session the assistants got up and left him alone with Collins. The Director turned off the cassette machine he had been using, gathered together the tapes upon which Seeler's story had been recorded, and placed them in a thick envelope which he sealed and signed. "That'll do." he said. "I'm starved. Seeler looked weary but he raised a smile. Stroking the straggly red beard still attached to his face, he said: "Give me a few minutes to wash up and I'll let you buy me dinner."

Collins leaned back on his chair and lit a cigarrette. "The old man is having a bash at The Carlton Club tonight. We'll let him stand for it." His eyes twinkled. "Why don't you go as you are - it'll give the boys a thrill. You know what the old man's like when it comes to undercover."

Seeler did not reply immediately. Collins studied him. "Is it the beard making you look old, or are you really that tired?"

Seeler stood, stretched out his arms, then sat again. "I really am that tired." Collins held out his cigarette. The big man accepted it and inhaled deeply. His shoulders relaxed, and he felt the tension still bleeding slowly from him. "I felt the strain on this one, Mike. You know I've never been keen on long term infiltration, and Northern Ireland is too close to home. This was the sort of job that makes you think about retiring."

There was a shrewd expression on Collins' face. "What did you leave out of the debrief?"

Seeler grinned. "No fooling you is there?" He lapsed briefly into silence. "I suppose I can tell you, old friend. I had to kill a couple of the wrong people." The forced note of levity could not hide his discomfort with the admission.

"Do you mean Philips and Murdoch?"

"Philips and a part-time copper named Mcgowan. I was present when they did Murdoch, but not active."

"And you don't want anyone in FIVE to know about it?"

"Not just FIVE, but anywhere in the SIS. I don't intend to let them have any kind of hold over me. Ever. The killing

McGowan would give them too much leverage."

Collins got to his feet and playfully punched his friend on the shoulder. "Your secret is safe with me. C'mon, the old man may be a bore but he entertains well. Come keep me company."

Seeler let himself be persuaded. "Okay, but don't complain if I leave early. I'm bushed."

The club was warm and conservative, with high ceilings and dusty chandeliers, wall panels of deep oak and dusty pictures in faded frames. Sir Alastair Watson was hosting a feast around a long table in a private dining room. Soup was being served when he interrupted one of his florid stories to greet Collins and Seeler. "Michael, my boy. Good to see you. I kept you a seat..." he waved to a chair. "And your colleague..." He peered hard at the big man. "It is Seeler, isn't it? Welcome old chap." He summoned a waiter. "An extra chair and a drink for our guest."

Mention of Seeler's name sent a thrill around the table. The big man was a legend; the world's most renowned intelligence operative; the man who spearheaded the routing of the european terrorist groups in the seventies. The most accomplished assasin on the planet. The gathering was made up of dreamers - bureaucrats who fantasised about covert action. But Seeler was the reality. The gunslinger. The yojimbo. The man they sent to get them out of trouble.

Through soup and over the entree Sir Alastair held sway, his stories interlaced, developing into a rambling monologue punctuated by loud guffaws as he laughed at his own punchlines. His voice, seasoned by quantities of gin, had taken on a rich, rolling timbre. Those around him laughed agreeably. His favours, or lack of them, could make or break a career. Few dared cross him. Even Collins, who had autonomy as head of CORE, and who was game for anything that kept the peace, laughed at the distended tales.

Over liquers Sir Alastair, looking smug and well ballasted, the tiny veins in his nose glowing red, began to discourse about a recent operation and an agent who had been doublecrossed by the department when he was considered unsalvageable. He hinted that Seeler's prescence that night had something to do with the case. The big man pricked up his ears at this indiscretion. He glanced at Collins and saw he was frowning.

"The upshot is," the old man was concluding, "The department really cannot lose. Either the Irish get him, ridding us of an unstable and potentially dangerous renegade, or he kills the members of the Republican cell and removes a serious threat to the greater good."

Collins decided it was time to try and curb the old man's loose tongue. Putting down his wine glass, he looked pointedly at Sir Alastair and noisily cleared his throat. He dabbed at the corners of his mouth with a napkin and fired a warning glance when the old man stared at him. One of the boys chirped up with a clever remark: "He could kill them and walk free. That would leave him still renegade, still unstable. How would that solve your problem?"

Steeped in his own cleverness, Sir Alastair winked. "I'm sure something could arranged. Right, Michael?" He grinned at the CORE Director, who seemed to be hovering on the verge of saying something caustic. As the implication sank in, a tremor went around the group." Summoning a waiter, the old man ordered a drink.

The evening wound to a natural ending. The guests made their excuses and filed out, each receiving a handshake and a personal word from the old man at the door. As Collins and Seeler moved to leave, Sir Alastair lowered his voice. "Would you chaps mind staying behind a minute? Just wait for me over at the table."

Once the three were alone in the room, Sir Alastair joined the other two around one end of the elongated table. Collins' disapproval was obvious as he waited for the old man to fill the void. He prepared to do so, but uncomfortably.

"Michael, I'd like to apologise for the gaff I made earlier this evening. The Congreave business, you know. Don't know quite what came over me. Old age, or the gin talking, what?" He was perspiring heavily in his embarassment. His brow shone. Collins muttered something about not minding, there was no harm done, but Seeler cut in."

"Then you ***were*** talking about Congreave?"

The old man's smile was sheepish. "Of course. In my foolishness I almost gave away a neat little set-up. My apologies to you too, old chap."

Seeler went on. "I must have misheard you. My understanding is that Congreave is out there trying to pre-empt a strike on his family, and the man with him is after revenge for an apparent IRA hit. But if what you are hinting at is correct, there's something not right about that story." Sensing a doublecross, he shot a fierce glance at Collins. "Were you in on this?"

"No. I was not."

"So," Seeler fixed the old man with that gaze of cold steel. "What's the tale?"

The old man diplomatically altered tack. "We have to go back a bit, to the time we received firm intelligence that the IRA, after a couple of quiet, and for them, frustrating years, were planning to make a big splash with the largest ever bombing campaign on the mainland. You know the background I'm sure; The Provos have reorganised brilliantly. Their cell system is the best protected on earth. The old guard are giving way to a newer, more radical, altogether more cold-blooded breed. This was an operation that if stopped, would cut the Provos to the core. Our information claimed that Finnbar Craig and Culum Strong were two of the cornerstones of the campaign. Our problem was that these people have never even been photographed. The pair of them masters at the art of staying hidden. We had little to go on, but we did have Congreave, an agent who had recently survived a confrontation with them. He was proving reluctant to help us, so I gave the order to have him back on the roster by an means necessary."

At mention of that phrase, Seeler's gaze, which had been watching his thumbs twiddle, darted up to lock onto Sir Alastair's face. The old man was still speaking. "As luck would have it, Dominic McGarrigle fell into our hands and we were able, through your expert infiltration, to accomplish the task without Congreave."

Seeler's face showed amazement as the incredible truth dawned on him. "By any means necessary....Are you telling me that YOUR people killed Jack Burt's family?"

The old man was having difficulty meeting Seeler's piercing stare. "Now that WAS an error."

Collins swallowed at the enormity of the admission. "I don't believe this."

Sir Alastair swallowed, and his adam's apple bobbed like a cork on a choppy sea. "Don't forget, until McGarrigle fell into our laps we had nothing. It was seen as essential we force Congreave's hand."

Seeler got up from his chair. "But you hit the wrong family?"

"That was a mistake - I freely admit it. Poor timing. The

agent who carried out the action has been ---"

"POOR TIMING? How can you sit there and..."

"NOW LISTEN TO ME!" boomed the old man. "This was a matter of expediancy. You understand that. You understand that better than anyone. Come on, man, you've never shied away from doing whatever was necessary." There followed a pause. The old man was breathing heavily. "Seeler, I know how this must sound, but believe me ---"

"I do believe you. This is classic British Intelligence. What I can't believe is that you stepped so far out of line. You sacrificed the lives of non-involved civilians. Even if you'd hit the right family there would have been no defence. And as for framing a terrorist group, putting the blame on the IRA..." He shook his head. "That was so naive, I'm surprised Congreave fell for it." Aghast at the facts, he covered his mouth with his hands. "You massacred an innocent family. Jesus."

Sir Alastair chewed uneasily on this assault. "Naive or not, Congreave did fall for it. And you have to admit it has all rather worked to our advantage. Impelled by Mr Burt, he is out to hit two important IRA men, and you have quite magnificently wrapped up a bagful of prize fish."

But Seeler was no longer listening. His expression had altered. Hardened. All emotion, every trace of it, had drained from his face as his thoughts were directed elsewhere. Glowering, he paced up and down, and when he spoke his voice was as taut as a bowstring. "Congreave and Burt will be after them. They're racing into a fight that isn't even theirs. They could get killed for nothing."

"Not for nothing." The old man said with a note of censure. "The political climate is changing. The PM can see that the Police involvement has run it's course. It won't be too long before FIVE assumes total responsibility for the situation in Northern Ireland." He paused, then said:"Seeler, have a drink. It's all water under the bridge."

"Don't patronise me. What do you know about being in action? What it does to a man?"

The old man reared stiffly. "May I remind you, young man, that from nineteen thirty nine to nineteen sixty one I was...."

"I know, I know, you won the war. You and John Wayne. But that was then and this is now." Turning on his heel he made for the door.

"Where are you going?"

Seeler halted at the door. He looked back. "I'm going to stop them, if I can. And you better pray I don't tell Jack Burt it was you had his family wiped out, or you may be seeing action again sooner than you thought!" The door slammed shut behind him.

Sir Alastair's piercing glare settled on the door. Collins, watching, was disturbed by what he saw on the old man's face.

"That man is out of control, Director!" Hissed Sir Alastair in a voice that was icily pompous. "You get him back on the leash!"

*

At the time that dawn began it's slow creeping over the horizon in the highlands of Scotland, and Sam escaped from the cottage with Congreave's family, Seeler loaded up his Range Rover and set off. It had taken until 3am to come up with the answer; PRISM. The camp run by former CORE operative David Parsons. The place, Murdoch had admitted under torture, where Anne Congreave and her children were in hiding. He recalled someone telling him that Finnbar had made a call.

He had begun by calling the hotel in Belfast, only to learn that the two men had checked out. He then contacted the local army intelligence unit and learned that Congreave had been informed of the death of Colonel Philips. Through the police he learned that Congreave had hired a private aircraft. A flight plan had been filed. The planned landing strip, he saw from a map, was one hundred miles east of PRISM. He telephoned the camp, and became worried when there was no reply. It was then he decided to act. Finnbar had settled on the revenge he imagined suitable for the death of Mary. He wanted a massacre, and Culum was being dragged along by the current.

Forcing the accelerator to the floor he watched the speedometer creep up to seventy miles per hour. There he let the needle on the dial hover. He would take no chances. If he was stopped for speeding, and the contents of the Rover discovered, he would be delayed. And since he had dared anger Sir Alastair, he could not rely on being quickly freed by the department. The old man made a spiteful enemy.

As daylight shouldered aside the night he found his second wind. It had been twenty four hours since he'd slept, but he was through the fatigue barrier and ready for the long drive.

Scotland, he mused. That meant rain!

It was late morning when Tim Healy of Special Branch paid Michael Collins a visit in his office. The two had known each other for years, and Healy had considered himself a friend of Seeler since a time, ten years earlier, when he and the big man had foiled an attempt on the life of the Queen in Horseguards parade. They never did anything great for each other, but Seeler and Healy were friends.

In appearance Healy could have been described as fatherly; tall, with stooped shoulders and a kindly face. Collins knew immediately that Healy had brought a problem. Healy never made social calls to the office. Taking a bottle of port and two glasses from a filing cabinet, Collins poured. "Cheers," he said, passing Healy a drink. The SB officer sniffed the liquid, then sipped.

"Not bad," he said. "But a bit unusual. I thought hardened secret agents were supposed to hide bottles of whisky in filing cabinets."

Collins smiled. "I've matured." He took to his chair. "What's up Tim?"

Healy squirmed until he was more comfortable on the chair. "I've been involved in the interrogation of the IRA men Seeler brought in. They're looking at some pretty serious charges. Lengthy prison terms."

"And...?"

"And one of them has indicated he wants to make a deal. In exchange for immunity, and possible relocation, he wants to give up the identity of the man who executed SAS Colonel Philips."

Though his face gave away nothing, Collins' mind was in a whirl. "Go on."

"Sir Alastair is keen. The interrogator has permission to deal. There's a great public relations coup at stake. You know how the establishment like to have someone they can crucify publicly when it comes to an issue as sensitive as this."

"What's your point, Tim?"

Healy raised an eyebrow. "You really want me to go through it? Okay. So far only three officers know the identity of the man who killed Philips. And of the three, two of us know that the man going to be named is Seeler. In disguise of course. If we are going to keep him and ourselves from becoming embroiled in an embarassing situation we have to come up with an answer."

Collins was dumbstruck. "You're right. Christ. The one thing we can't do is compromise Seeler. If we allow that to happen we'll lose a lot of credibility with other operatives. This business is tough enough. Ideas?"

"Nothing yet. But we need an answer pretty quickly. The interrogator has an appointment to brief his department head this afternoon. As things stand, even if we move quickly at least a half dozen people will know of Seeler's part in the operation. And as you know, he hates anyone knowing about his work."

Collins was already seeking a solution. "What if we don't mention Seeler. Why not just slot the real Dominic into the picture?"

"What do you mean?"

"Re-do the paperwork. Dominic was already there at the cellars. Just alter the date of his intake. Let him take the fall for Seeler."

"What about the matter of identification? I'm sure Seeler did a good job, but at some point the IRA man will be asked to pick him out and the hole will appear."

Collins gave a grim smile. "Then we'll have to take a more draconian outlook."

"You mean stitch up the real Dominic?"

"That's pretty much what I mean. Can you do it?"

Healy paused for thought. "With a little care, a little manipulation, I ought to be able to make it. Yes, I'm pretty sure I can."

32:

A blanket of slate-grey cloud slid over the horizon and approached with visible speed. "Rain coming." Jack muttered. It was late afternoon, and the day had been a strain. For hours he and Congreave had been creeping through thick woodland, ever fearful, scared and sweating, darting looks at every odd sound, and the woods were full of odd sounds.

The calm was, perhaps, the most disturbing thing of all. The greatest strain. They had found no sign of the Irish trio. Though the sun shone, the temperature was falling. The slight wind that did manage to reach them through the undergrowth was damp and cutting. Despite their bravest efforts the two men could not help but feel a little disheartened.

"Let's sit a while." Jack proposed. He pointed to his right, where the edge of the forest could be discerned. "Over here should do."

Earlier in the day Colin had used the tiny primus stove he had found in the backpack and made hot coffee, the bulk of which he stored in a thermos flask. Now he emptied the flask into two plastic mugs and they each drank. They were still jumpy; they had been sure the Irishmen would doubleback and try to hit them. Jack said, aloud, and with hope: "Maybe they decided on a clean getaway. We could do the same."

Congreave was unconvinced. "You heard the taunts Jack. You know they've not gone away. They know we're as stuck as they are. Probably they want to rest up and hit us at night."

"I wish we had a better line of defence. I wouldn't mind them following us back to PRISM. There I could make a stand. Let them come on our terms."

"Forget it. We're here until Sam comes to get us."

Colin sipped at his drink. "You ought to be used to this waiting around. After Vietnam."

Jack nodded. "Still doesn't make it any easier."

Colin grinned. "Did you spend much of the time out on patrol?"

"Yeah, too much. Wrecked by fear in the field and wrecked by drink and dope in the base." He rolled his shoulders to ease the tension. "Christ, I feel so old when I think about those days. Nineteen seventy three I was last there."

"Didn't you ever think of dodging the draft?"

Jack shook his head. "No way. I was a volunteer. I still don't understand why. I do know I'm as scared now as I was then; and at that time I was married to my first wife and had a baby son. I didn't see him until he was fourteen months old. There were moments where I believed I was going to die, and I was so angry that I might never get to see the boy I got up and fought back."

"The anger carried you through." Colin remarked in a voice that said he understood. "If you were a volunteer, why didn't you get out?"

"Like I said, there's so much I don't understand. Some kind of inbred exaggerated loyalty to my country. My dad was strong on fighting for America. He lost a leg in Korea."

"You have any family left?"

"No...not a soul."

"Your son, your first wife?"

"He died in '83."

"I'm sorry Jack." Colin said quickly.

"There was no reason for it really. He was driving home one night when a drunk crossed the centre of the road and hit him head on." His voice lowered to a near-whisper. It was plain the memory still hurt.

Colin chanced a look around. He had to be cautious he did not get so absorbed in the tale he became careless. "What about your first wife?"

"I last saw Angela in '83. At the funeral. She had a new life by then. We had nothing to say to each other. I had just married Carol." He paused, sadly, then went on:
"It was almost as though we'd never known each other." He looked away from the massed trees, at the hillsides, and silently wished he could just walk away.

Colin, as if reading his thoughts, said: "If we tried to get back without Sam we'd be at it for hours. This is Sam's terrain. He'll find us."

Jack upturned his near empty cup onto the grass. "I just don't want to sit here like a coconut in a shy."

"Nor me, but ---"
Colin was interrupted by the crackling of the walkie talkie hooked into one of his jacket pockets.

"Are you there, lads?"
Colin snatched the handset to his mouth and depressed the send button. "Sam? We're fine. Is everything all right? Where are you?"
"I'm fine. The cargo reached base safely. The journey was longer than I anticipated - the kids were worn out. I hated leaving them but I had to come for you. I'm at the cottage, where are you?"

Colin quickly described their location. Sam knew it.
"I'll be with you in a few minutes. What's the situation like?"
"Still tense. Not resolved."
"I'll be right down. Keep your eyes peeled."

They waited for what seemed an interminable period. Then a small figure tramped into view over the crest of the hill. Sam. His pack bobbing on his back as he hurried downhill. Colin moved to the edge of the trees, putting himself in clear view to guide Sam. He waved as a single shot boomed. Sam halted at the sound, then began to run frantically, his arms pumping. Colin and Jack were up instantly, guns ready, searching for the origin of the shot. Sam still seemed an impossible distance away.

"C'mon Sam. Go for it." Jack muttered as Sam descended the hillside in leaping bounds. Then a second shot reverberated throughout the dank woodland, the sound echoing along the mountain corridors.

Sam fell. He had been moving almost uncontrollably fast and now he tumbled headlong and rolled, limply, arms flailing at impossible angles as he spun. His head jolted as it struck rock.

"Jesus." Jack hissed, voice warped with anger and fear. They watched in horror as Sam's lifeless body cartwheeled to a dead halt only yards away. On impulse Jack moved to help him, but Colin grasped his arm. "Wait."

Jack was breathing nasally. "At least we know they are still around." His mouth was dry. Warily he scanned the surrounding area, but the trees were too close for him to see any great distance. "They must have someone in the treetops. They knew we were strangers and that we'd need someone to guide us out. Now we're pinned down here." His voice was guttural, a note of desperation creeping in. The waiting had been hard.

Colin heaved a sigh. "The battle lines are drawn. If we want out of here we'll have to fight."

Jack clenched a fist. His face was resolute. "That's why we're here." His rubbed his hands on the thick lining of his jacket, then shouldered his pack and took a firm grip on his pistol. "We can't go back. I vote we hunt bear in the woods."

"You're the jungle fighter. You take point. I'll be right

behind you."

Jack gave a wry smile."You're all heart." They shared a nervous laugh. Then a shrill cry cut the air and froze the laughter in their throats. An animal screeching, but not from any animal. "Congreave! I'm gonna have your balls Congreave! Come and get it!"

Jack was tense, poised on the balls of his feet. Then something heavy crashed through the undergrowth and he spun, finger on the trigger, and loosed a series of gunshots until the gun clicked empty. He stood, feeling slightly foolish, breathing heavily, the gun still in his outstretched hand. Beside him, Colin had dropped into a crouch. He warily eyed the surroundings. "Reload," he whispered. "I'll cover. If you have to shoot again, do it in bursts of three rounds. We're not carrying an arsenal."

Apologising, Jack dropped to one knee to reload. "Guess I'm getting a little hinky."

"Don't tell me your personal problems." Congreave's tone was harsh, the initial hostility between them resurfacing once the pressure was on, a reminder that they were not together through choice.

Jack ignored the remark. "They're close. Close enough to throw a rock. Even worse, they know where we are. We can't afford to get lazy."

A faint gasp froze them to the spot. Colin cried out: "Sam!" He hurried to the stricken man's side and dragged him into the cover of the trees. He shot a glance at Jack. "Keep your eyes open. I'll tend to him."

He bent over the body and examined the wounds. The gunshot had put a small hole square in the centre of Sam's chest, but the blood from it was not as much as might have been expected. Colin took that as a bad sign. Bleeding was internal. His arms lay at unnatural angles - both broken, and his face was badly scuffed. But he was breathing, and his eyes were open. Colin fitted a hand under Sam's neck to raise him. "How are you doing, Sam?"

Sam tried to speak, but in the attempt sputtered flecks of blood onto his face. His face was bloodlessly white, and his lips were stretched into a humourless grin. He took a great wheezing breath. "I've felt better!" He tried to laugh, but collapsed into a fit of painful coughing. He seemed to take forever to gather his strength to speak again. "They're safe, Colin lad. Back at the camp. Good kids....did the best I could. Just make sure you get there first."

"I will." Colin promised. "You rest now. We're going to get you out of this."

Sam's laugh crumbled into a groan of pain. Bravely he faced the inevitable. "Don't kid a kidder, eh, kid? I seen wounds like this before. They're survivable, but not in the wilds. Not without good medical kit. I..." he averted his face as pain bit. "COLIN!!!" the cry was wrested from him.

"What Sam, what?"

"......get them...." his voice tailed away to a sigh, and his head flopped to one side. Colin gently lowered him to the ground. When he looked up at Jack his eyes were flint-hard.

He rose from his crouch, then flipped open his pack and rummaged inside. Jack asked him what he was doing. "Just seeing exactly what Sam packed for us. It's time we went on the offensive."

*

It was late afternoon when Michael Collins got the message to meet Healy at The Cellars. They conferred in a locked office. Collins asked Healy what was wrong, "Why did I have to get here so quickly?"

"If we want to keep Seeler out of jail we have to move within the hour. The man who wants the deal, his name is Ivan Thomas. He's in his mid twenties, runs a couple of legit businesses and, according to his story, he's been one of three main IRA weapons feeds these past four years. He's getting his deal this afternoon. I've altered the paperwork on Dominic McGarrigle, but we owe Seaton a favour."

"That creep. I'm surprised he fell in line."

"I also had to confide in Sir Alastair Watson. He sanctioned the move. As far as Ivan's brief is concerned, when Ivan sees Dominic this afternoon he'll be identifying the man he saw kill Colonel Peter Philips."

Collins looked grave. "Seeler won't like this many people knowing the truth."

"There was no other way to legitimise the alterations. This way everyone is covered. The chain of command has moved to protect one of it's footsoldiers."

"But it means we owe people."

Healy shrugged. "Sometimes compromise is the only way to get a thing done."

Collins said nothing further. He knew with what glee Sir Alastair would have ordered the cover-up. He would have Seeler in his pocket, one of the few men in the department who did not fear him was going to be in his debt. Seeler was back on the leash.

He sighed. "Okay, so what happens next?"

"The legal process is rolling. This afternoon Ivan will make a statement and formerly identify McGarrigle. Then it's time to go public, give the government's Irish policy a shot in the arm and splinter the Provos organisation. It's going to be a tabloid editor's dream. Headlines galore."

"But what about McGarrigle? He and Seeler are not an exact match. What if Ivan spots a rat?"

"We have the clothes Seeler wore, and we can cut Dominic's hair to make him look the part. From fifteen feet, and with the entire deal and Ivan's freedom hinging on the positive ID, I'd say that Ivan will deliver."

"What about Dominic? He'll have a lawyer. What will he say when he gets to court?"

"He'll never get to court. There'll be a guilty plea and a petition for clemency, the usual rigmarole about political crime being different. For reasons of security he'll not have to attend. And his lawyer will be one of Sir Alastair's 'people'."

"Sounds like the old man's got it all worked out."

"Credit where it's due, Mike. This kind of stuff is what he's good at."

"And what does it cost us? What is Ivan's part of the deal?"

Healy grimaced. "Slap on the wrist. Supergrass status. New name, new place of residence. An income for life."

"Bastard."

"In exchange, Seeler doesn't get nailed and we keep him on our side. That's how it goes."

There was a pause. From a pocket Healy took a pipe and a pouch stuffed with aromatic tobacco. He filled the pipe bowl, lit a match and puffed contentedly, flooding the room with a sweet, woody odour. "Better get going, I suppose. I have to persuade Dominic to clean up and get into Seeler's old clothes."

"Poor bastard won't know what's hit him once the process starts." Collins murmured. Healy took the pipe from his mouth. His face frowned. "That poor bastard has been killing, and training killers for the best part of twenty years. His reward has been a long time coming, but he's going to get it." He sucked on his pipe. "I better be going. I'll keep you posted."

He left the office leaving Collins alone with his thoughts.

*

33:

Seeler had driven without respite the whole day, pausing only briefly to re-fuel and buy coffee and sandwiches. He had visited PRISM numerous times and had no difficulty finding the camp, even though he covered the last few miles in the gloom of twilight. He made his approach with the headlamps off, cutting the engine and coasting to a halt just outside the gates. Then taking a favoured weapon - a Browning Hi-power pistol, and spare ammunition clips, he crept into the compound.

Moving with extreme stealth he quickly made a tour of the nearest buildings, checking the interiors until he was able to eliminate them from his thinking. His path took him, almost naturally, to the gymnasium where he found Parsons' body still bound to the pillar. Dead over twenty four hours, the blood that caked him had dried hard and black, and his skin, where blood had drained away, was a horrid, deathly grey.

Seeler had never been superstitious, but he did harbour, somewhere deep inside himself, the idea that there must be a God. To this God he offered a silent prayer on Parsons behalf and then, all business, he made a mental note to return with a knife to cut the body free. He made for the remaining building, the cottage situated at the north east corner of the camp.

Lights were on in the cottage. One downstairs, one up. He knocked on the door. From beyond he could almost sense the fear gathering as Anne listened. Then he heard her call in a tremulous voice. "Who's there?"

"Anne, you may not remember me but we have met. My name is Seeler. I'm here to help."

"Step away from the door," she called out, still fighting

for control. "I have a gun."

He obediantly took a backward step. The door opened an inch and Anne's face, crouched behind the fat double barrels of a shotgun, peered at him. Her face was haggard and drawn, her cheeks hollow craters, dark in the half light. Her hair hung in lank strands. But it was the eyes Seeler looked to. He saw that she recognised him, and he smiled. "May I come in?"

"It is you, isn't it?" she whispered, her voice lost in a whirlwind of relief. "Seeler, it is you. Come in. Come in."

He stepped inside and locked the door. She was still strung taut, though she did lower the muzzle of the shotgun, aiming the barrels at the floor when they talked. She asked him if he had any news of Colin, and her face fell when he replied he did not. "That doesn't mean there's something wrong." he hurried to assure her. "Colin's one of the best. He'll take some stopping."

She tried to remain calm, but she was plainly shaken. "Let me get you something to eat and drink." she said mechanically, putting down the shotgun and turning for the kitchen. She had spent hours taking refuge in there, cleaning up, over and over, shielding herself beneath a cowl of industry.

He let her work; knowing it was a necessary purgative. She cooked a meal and served him. After he had eaten he tried to persuade her to talk. This she did, haltingly at first then with increasing fluidity as she unburdened herself of the fears. Afterwards she seemed better for it and thanked him for listening. He shrugged; it was nothing. She asked him if he was sure the camp was empty. When he nodded, she said she might go out for some air.

He was thinking. "You said Sam left here just after

lunch?" She nodded. "Then, depending on how long it took him to find Colin and Jack, he might have been back by now."

"Something is wrong." She said. "I just know it."

Her face started to contort as anxieties surged afresh. He put out a hand and grasped her fingers. "He's fine, believe me. And you're going to have him back."

She swallowed, hard, and a fat tear overflowed and ran down her cheek. "I wish I could believe that."

He pulled out a hankerchief and pressed it upon her, urging her to wipe her eyes.

At last she seemed to settle. She asked him what he was going to do next. He was beginning to feel the full weight of fatigue lean on him. "Well, I'm going to make up a pack and go out to look for him. But before I do that I'm going to put you in my care and send you and the kids out of here."

"Is that safe?"

He smiled."It will be if you can drive." She smiled back. She was looking better. "But before that," he said, "I need a favour from you."

She raised an eyebrow in inquiry. "I'll do anything I can to help. What is it you want?"

"I've been awake a full thirty six hours. Now I can stay awake, but if I'm to be sharp when I go out there I ought to get some sleep. If you'll stay awake until I'm ready I promise I'll have you out of here the first moment I can. Will you do that?"

"I'll be glad to. I feel so much safer just having you here. Colin told me so much about ----" she halted, face flushed with embarassment. "I'm sorry. I know he shouldn't have mentioned anything about work. But when a man works with danger I think it helps if he has a sympathetic ear at home, or a friend to lean on. And we've always been very close."

He smiled. "No problem." he felt a yawn coming on. As his mouth flexed open, he stretched out his arms. "I'll get my head down now. The sooner I sleep the sooner I'll get up again. May I?" He indicated the bedroom. She nodded. "Of course, what time shall I wake you?"

He glanced at his watch. "It's nine. No point my walking in the night. Wake me at four. That way I can be out at first light, and you'll have the whole day to get down to London."

"Why London?"

But he was already at the bedroom door. "Tell you later," he called over his shoulder. "See you at four."

He was asleep the moment his head struck the pillow. Dreamless, or at least, undisturbed sleep. Until some distant sound wormed it's way into his mind and began to jangle alarm bells. The sound rang out again, and he knew it was a cry for help. An extended, agonised scream. He stirred with a leaden murmur, then the cry came again, louder this time, no longer clouded by sleep, and he was on his feet in an instant. His entire body reverberated with the shock of sudden fright, but he recovered quickly and, taking his gun, hurried outside.

He took no chances. He had survived this long by being careful, and he was careful now. Every corner was examined before he rounded it, and he refused to be rushed even by the urgent screams coming from the centre of the camp. Anne was in trouble, but if he was killed rushing in he would be of no use to her. Then the screams subsided.

He found his way to the gymnasium. Realisation hit him full force and he cursed; he should have warned her about Parsons. Relaxing slightly he put away the gun and walked into the gym. Anne was on her knees, in a position of supplication, at the feet of the dead man. Her head was down, her hair covering her face, but he could hear her snuffling. Gently he placed an arm around her shoulders and coaxed her to her feet. She fell against him and cried with her face buried in his shirt. He led her back to the cottage and gave her coffee. She sat for a lengthy period, staring into space, giving only murmured, monosyllabic replies to his questions. He apologised for not warning her, and she accepted this with a dip of her head.

It was midnight. His own excitement was sinking and weariness making itself known. Seeing him stifle a yawn, guilt cut into her and she became animated. She got to her feet and herded him into the bedroom, insistent she would wake him at the correct time. He did not argue, and in minutes he was asleep.

Anne dutifully seated herself on a hardbacked chair and placed the shotgun at her side. The night was cold, and she wrapped a shawl around her shoulders to fend off the chill. In the second bedroom she heard one of her children sleeptalking. She fought the heaviness of her eyelids, forced herself to remain alert, but soon, without being aware of it, was falling into a deep sleep.

*

It had been a long night, fraught with bureaucratic pitfalls, but Healy was at last in the clear. He opened the cell door and stepped into the small, windowless cubicle. The odour of perspiration assaulted his olfactory senses, and the heat, turned up to wear down the morale of the inmates, made him want to peel off a couple of layers.

Dominic was seated on the edge of the bunk. Hands linked calmly together as he waited. For all his control, disquiet still shone on his face. He watched Healy step into the cell. "What next?" he growled. He remained unconvinced about the change of clothes and the trimming of hair and beard.

"Time to move." Healy said cheerily. "You look better."

"Different is all, not better. What are you up to, you bastards?"

Healy feigned surprise. "I was under the impression you'd been told. We are having to move you out. I just thought this was a good time for a clean up and a few new clothes. I know the bathing facilities have not been too good here."

Dominic was staring at him in a baleful, distrustful manner. Healy met the stare, unflinching, and at length Dominic turned away.

"I've a couple of guards in the corridor. Shall we go?" He moved aside to allow Dominic to pass. The big boned man rose slowly, as though by great effort, and took the first step. In the corridor he allowed himself to be handcuffed and was marched along the corridor.

"Where are we going?"

"I told you. Somewhere safe." Healy replied tartly. The small group rounded a corner. Another, identical corridor faced them, a long whitewashed tunnel brightly lit by glaring flourescent tubes. Dominic stopped dead and glowered down at Healy. "Save your smart-arse answers, I want to know where we are going?"

Healy looked annoyed. "To a house in the country. Like I said, a place where your worthless hide will be safe. Okay now?"

Dominic continued to glower. "Why do I need to be kept safe? I made a deal with you bastards. Is this some kind of Brit doublecross? Is it?" His arms strained against the cuffs that locked his hands behind him. Healy was glad the man was manacled. He remained calm."Quite correct. You *did* make a deal. Everything went according to plan and as a result a number of your contemporaries are now in here. Does that explain why we can't keep you here?"

Dominic breathed in to stifle his ire. Without another word he started walking again, catching the guards by surprise. They quickly caught up. The seemingly endless corridor ended, turning abruptly right into a small reception area.

A group of men, four uniformed guards and a small man, apparently a prisoner, stood watching their approach. The prisoner was of medium height, in his mid-twenties with cropped hair and a pale, gaunt face. He was thin, dressed in a tatty sweater, grimy jeans and heavy boots. His eyes stared vacantly at the big man as he approached. Dominic looked into the eyes, saw a flicker of uncertainty, then the man appeared to gather his nerve and he spoke aloud. "Hello Dominic."

Dominic glowered. There was a trick here, somewhere. All his instincts screamed at him. Ignoring the other prisoner he stalked past, muttering at Healy: "You bastards, you let him see me on purpose. I'm not a fool. You're setting me up!"

"Just wanted you to know I was telling you the truth." Healy responded. He stopped by a wooden door. He knocked, then pushed the door open. "In here."

"Now what?"

"Someone to see you. We have a few details to be ironed out."

Dominic' s frown intensified. "If you're messing me about, I'll....." If he hadn't been handcuffed he would have shook a fist in Healy's face. Instead, he stepped into the room. The door was closed behind him, and he found himself facing a desk of deep oak, behind which sat a man in an expensive suit. His hair was silvery, and neatly kept. He was scribbling rapidly, head down, face hidden .A comfortable looking chair upholstered in leather stained a rich ox-blood colour sat vacant before the desk. Dominic lowered himself onto the chair and settled down to wait.

The man put down the pen and looked up. He gave a terse, professional smile. "Good evening to you. My name is John Penworthy. I'm here to be your legal representative."

"Would you mind telling me what's going on? Why do I need you?"

"You are facing rather serious charges."

"Charges?"

"Yes. You are to be detained under the Prevention of Terrorism Act, and are to be charged with the murder of a British soldier."

Dominic's face showed his fury. "Bastards. Just when and where am I supposed to have killed this soldier?"

"Three days ago, in Belfast."

Dominic chuckled. "Bastards. I've been held here for nearly six weeks. I've not been in Belfast for fifteen years."

"Well I'm here to help you with your defence. Give me your side of the story and I'll do my best."

Dominic stood locked in rage for long minutes, then when he had gathered his determination he slowly sat down. Once he started to talk the words flowed.

Healy turned away from the door and at a sluggish pace walked back to the reception area. At the desk a guard in uniform sat watching a bank of six closed circuit television monitors. Beyond the desk was a heavy door marked with the word *Supervisor* on a plaque. Healy knocked on this door and entered. Inside, Seaton and Sir Alastair broke off their conversation to look at him.

"Ah, Healy," Sir Alastair greeted him cordially. "Everything in order, I take it?"

"McGarrigle is in with his Brief now." Healy remarked."So far it's all going to plan."

"Excellent. Have you spoken to Director Collins?"

"He's been fully appraised, Sir, if that's what you mean."

"That's exactly what I mean." Lifting the telephone receiver, the old man dialled the private number of the CORE Director. Collins picked up on the second ring. Sir Alastair rapidly summarised the situation, adding: "Discussion of the affair is to remain restricted, no more than we four to know about it, is that understood?" Though he was speaking to Collins, he looked to Seaton and Healy for confirmation. The men nodded. "Okay then, Michael. I'll be seeing you. Oh, one more thing. Have you spoken to Seeler yet? Well, when he returns, have him pop in to see me will you? There's a good chap. I might have a little job for him. Goodnight." Putting down the receiver, he beamed. "Well, a satisfactory nights' work."

In his office, Collins cradled the receiver to his cheek. His stare was cold. Seeler was hooked now. The old man would systematically reel him in, make him part of what he called his *Private Portfolio.* Poor bastard.

How he hated that old man!

34:

Leaving Sam's body, Colin and Jack hastened along a zigzagging path that took them deeper into the forest. Knowing the Irishmen must keep track of them or lose the advantage, they moved quickly, making no attempt at stealth, hoping that in their haste the followers might grow careless and reveal themselves. As they ran, sweat poured from them; Jack set a cracking pace and Colin, despite being very fit, this time found it hard to keep up.

Within a couple of hours dusk started to filter through the cool verdant deep of the woodland, dappling the ground with bright patches of gold. In a clearing, the air heavy with damp, and buzzing with midges, Jack called a halt and sat with his back to a tree. Colin dropped gratefully beside him.

"Could you go for a drink?" Jack asked, sweat dripping from the tip of his nose. Colin swallowed dryly. He nodded. Jack tugged a flask from his pack. Unscrewing the cap, he upturned it to use as a cup. He poured, and the coffee aroma sweetened the dank, musty air. They drank in a spirit of quiet comradeship. Being together, and experiencing the feeling of going *through* something together, forged a bond. One thing was becoming clear; they could rely on each other.

Jack downed his coffee quickly, then got to his feet and rummaged in his pack. "I vote we spend the night here," he said. "So I'll make a few preparations." Colin nodded, glad to be resting. He shrugged off his pack and unbuttoned his thick jacket. "I must have lost four or five pounds sweating in this gear. What do you have there?"

Jack held up a spool of thin wire. "The trip wires you found earlier. You have to hand it to Sam, he brought us well prepared." He moved away to a spot a few metres beyond the edge of the clearing and began to thread a perimeter. He looped the wire around trees at ankle height, and, when he was done, returned to the centre of the clearing. Dusk had passed, and the gloom between dusk and full night was dense enough to strain the eyes.

"We'll be okay here," Jack whispered. "The perimeter covers a radius of about fifty metres. As long as one of us stays on watch and is careful, they won't surprise us." He looked at Colin, thought he could make out a grin in the gloom. "What?"

"You. You seem so at home suddenly."

Jack managed a smile. "Funny how it all comes back. The night moves. Keeping quiet, picking a good spot. Listening to the night." He paused, aware that the sounds of the forest were undergoing a subtle change. Day creatures were now quiet, to be replaced by the shuffling of nocturnals.

The earth on which they sat was thickly matted with generations of fallen leaves. They divided up a ration pack, barely speaking as they ate. Colin set up the primus and soon they had more hot coffee.

"In Vietnam, some of the people hunting us, the hardcore NVA, were so good they could smell us if we chewed gum. The smell of coffee would have brought them from miles around."

"Did you see much action?"

Jack nodded. "Someone once said something about the best of times, the worst of times. That's how it was for me. It was hell, but having survived it I can say I wouldn't have missed it for the world. I made the best buddies a man ever had. I learned about friendship, death, and the incompetance and corruption of any massive organisation. I saw fuck-ups on an enormous scale. While we were being blown up by our own guys, others seemed to spend all their time ripping off Uncle Sam. Selling PX stuff to the natives and taking massive profits. Real Milo Minderbinder, Catch-22 stuff. I learned to grieve, and to value friends."

Colin said, acidly. "That's not exactly the conventional wisdom for Vietnam vets. Usually all we get to hear is the story of the ruined lives, the high rates of alcoholism, suicide and drug taking."

Jack was grave. "I know guys those things happened to. Over there and after we came back. I guess I was lucky. What else can I say?"

Colin poured refills. They lapsed into near silence. When words were exchanged they did little to mask the discomfort they felt, sitting exposed and vulnerable in a hostile environment.

"You nervous?" Colin muttered. Jack waved away a bug that danced on his face, and the luminous hands of his wristwatch flitted eerily like a firefly as his hand moved.

"Yes I'm nervous. I hate sitting here. I hate having to stop. But if we keep moving at night we'll end up lost. Listen." They both listened intently, but the only sounds were the buzzing of the nightlife.

"Nothing." Colin murmured. Jack peered at him in the deepening gloom. "Exactly. By forcing the pace I'd hoped we'd force them into the open. If they were rushing we'd hear them coming."

"So either they have lost us, or they are smart enough to come after us slow. What do we do now?"

"We stay here tonight. We have to rest sometime. If we had to face them tired we'd stand less of a chance." There was a pause, then Jack told Colin to get some sleep. "I'll take the first watch and wake you in three hours."

"You'll be okay?"

Jack held up a hand. The night was now so thick Colin could barely distinguish the movement. The American was holding one end of the wire. "This wire's very thin and totally black. If they walk into it - and if they're coming they will, I'll feel the tug on this end. Believe me, I'll give you a kick when that happens."

Colin could hear the grim humour in Jack's tone. The man was alright, he told himself, and retreating to a corner of the clearing he curled up and closed his eyes. He did not remember falling asleep, but when he next peered at the backlit face of his watch almost two hours had passed. He sat up. The air felt thick, unnaturally damp, and his face tickled as sweat ran down it. A gentle wafting breeze was just discernible, but not strong enough to relieve the humidity.

While Colin had slept, Jack had taken a lamp from his pack. It sat beside him now, it's soft glow bathing his profile in a gentle, flattering light. Colin wiped his sleeve across his brow and eased himself upright. Jack seemed absorbed, unaware of Colin's quiet approach, and when the Englishman saw what Jack was studying, he understood why.

He had photographs on his lap. Family pictures. Colin lowered himself to the ground, and when Jack, suddenly aware of his prescence, turned to look at him, his eyes were glinting mistily. He started to talk about his family, the loss and the loneliness, but his voice, though oddly emotionless, had a jaggedness to it, like the deadly edge of a rusting sawblade.

"S'funny, sitting here like this, alone in the night. I just realised I've hardly given Carol and the kids a thought today. This whole thing is about them, and what happened, and yet I've been so obsessed I let them slip out of sight."

He lapsed into silence and sat, isolated, with his thoughts. Beside him, Colin, chewing absently on his lower lip, found himself thinking about Anne. The knowledge that she and the children were safe comforted him. Almost before he knew it he heard himself saying aloud: "You feel guilty?"

Jack looked puzzled. "I don't know about guilt. I feel anger, I do know that. It's come on like a slow burn, but now it's here it's not going to go away." He closed the fingers of one hand into a fist. "I'm going to have those sons of bitches. I feel unstoppable, Colin, and that scares me. I'm afraid of what I might do if I blow."

"I know that feeling."

Jack looked at him in surprise. "What do you mean?"

"Well, you're under pressure, distanced from what's happening around you. You feel unplugged from reality. It's like....you're attached to the world through some switchboard arrangement, and as the pressure on you grows, the plugs that make the connections keep getting pulled out. One after another. Out they come. You get scared that the very last plug will be pulled and you'll lose your grasp. You can't see further than the moment you're existing in. And that's scary."

Jack nodded, as if given the answer to some impossible riddle. The two men felt close. Then Jack broke the mood by glancing at his watch and exclaiming. "Hey, what are you doing up? It's not your time yet."

"I've slept long enough. You get your head down. I'll spell you."

"I am tired," Jack said through a yawn. He got to his feet, his knees popping audibly, and picked up his sleeping bag. In minutes he was asleep, and immediately plunged into a dream.

He was in his car, driving south along a deserted stretch

of highway when he saw a small group of figures on the shoulder. There was something familiar about them, the woman, the two children. They were waving, and he was almost level with them before he recognised their faces. It was Carol, and the kids. And even the recognition came as a shock, for he realised he'd forgotten what they really looked like. He'd clung to the photographs, and he now knew they were not quite right.

He sped past them, braked hard and began to steer onto the shoulder, but the car would not respond. Frantically he pumped the pedal with his foot, but the car did not slow. With a loud curse he yanked on the handbrake, heard it pull taut with a serrated, rasping sound. It failed. He glanced in the mirror and saw the figures shrinking as he left them behind. They were still waving. He raged in desperation, pleading with the car to stop....

Colin saw him moving in his sleep. Jack murmured. Tried to reach out to his family. Called Carol's name.

Shutting off the lamp, Colin settled down to wait.

*

Seeler woke with a start. His heart was pounding, and for long moments he struggled to know where he was. Groping for the bedside lamp he blinked in the sudden glare and peered at his wristwatch. The sky outside the window was showing the first faint promise of day; four am. He dressed, and crept into the lounge. Anne was there, sleeping soundly on a chair by the bay window. The shotgun on her lap. He smiled wryly, then went into the kitchen and made himself tea and toast. He was eating when Anne walked in. She had put down the gun.

There was an embarassed flush to her face. She apologised for sleeping, and was relieved at his calm acceptance of her slip. When they had eaten, they carried the still sleeping children, wrapped in blankets, out to the car. Seeler packed Anne into the Range Rover and gave her money. "Here, this should cover any expenses on the way down."

She leaned out of the driver's window and smiled at him. Her face was still haggard with worry, but there was hope there too. "Thank you for everything." she said. "I can't tell you how much you've helped."

"That's okay. You have my address, you have my key and the instructions about turning off the alarm in the flat. You can answer the phone - I'll probably call you. Got all that?" She said she had. She gunned the engine, and it was with relief he watched the taillights of the Rover vanish over the dark horizon. He glanced skywards, saw the still faint onset of dawn, and knew that despite his tiredness he had to be moving. Trudging back indoors he broke into the locker room and packed a rucksack. Cracking open a weapons cabinet he armed himself with gun and knife. Then taking a map he marked the route to the cottage - which he had visited before, and left.

At the gate he paused to look ahead, at the dark rolling bulk of the hills. It would be light within two to three hours, and it was time he was gone. As he trudged he felt elation. Whatever the outcome, whatever lay ahead, it felt good to be breathing clean air. The silence too was healing, after the constant irritation of city noise. He began to enjoy the exertion of walking. He enjoyed the chase, the adrenal surge of action, and he viewed the imminent confrontation with a feeling of exhilaration.

He walked the mossy earth, his eyes on the distance, his mind on survival, his senses sweeping, sweeping.

35:

His powers fuelled by the night, Finnbar was at home as any nocturnal. Hour after hour he drove Culum and the wounded Norm at a slow but relentless pace, soundlessly trailing his quarry. Step by step they cautiously covered the ground. Whenever a voice was raised in protest he silenced it with the force of his vehemence. He stopped dead once when he spied a pinprick of light to his left, but it had vanished before he could properly fix it's position. On gut instinct he steered towards the spot he believed it to be. Norm grumbled, and in a flash Finn had spun around and grasped him by the throat."Listen," he hissed. "We're here to do what we came for. So shut it!"

He was ready to hit out, but Culum coolly inserted himself between the two men. "I've got him," he muttered soothingly to Finnbar. "Everything's okay, I've got him." Releasing Norm, Finn turned away. Slowly Culum levered Norm upright and brushed him down. Then he glanced at the dark shadow he would not have recognised had he not known it was Finnbar.

"The man needs a rest, Finn. What are you trying to do, run us into the ground? If we stumble into Congreave in this state he'll be laughing as he mops us up."

"I'm not tired." Finn replied flatly. He tried to contain his impatience, but when he heard Norm grunt in pain, he felt a flush of fury. Reaching out he grasped Norm by the collar and hauled him forward until their faces were only inches apart. "Don't make me hurt you Norm!"

"Finnbar..." Culum said softly. "This is Norm. He's one of us. Think about what you are doing. Maybe we should take a break."

Finnbar inhaled deeply, filled his chest, and had a flash of reason. He decided to relent. "Ten minutes." he said, "then I'll be back down here for you both."

While Culum and Norm sank to the ground, and Culum dug in a backpack he had stolen from PRISM for food and cans of cold drinks, Finn moved ahead, gently parting the curtain of branches. As he moved, his head seemed filled by the pounding of his heart and the twittering of the forest creatures. The sense of reason had deserted him, and his thoughts rotated around the vicious impulses that drove him. Congreave; he had to die. And Finn would probably have to do the work himself. Norm had never been more than a glorified driver, and Cully, Cully was not the same man anymore. He had lost heart the day Congreave killed Mary.

Impatiently he returned to his two companions. "Let's be moving." He growled.

Culum started to protest, but his tone was weak. He had lost the will to resist Finnbar and was silenced by a wild eyed glare he felt, rather than saw, beaming at him in the intense gloom. His worst fears were realised. Finn had gone completely animal.

"We go on." He said simply.

Finn led them once more. His posture surging forward, his eyes wide and scanning, his hands gently brushing aside overhanging branches. He moved smoothly, felt himself gaining momentum, a growing excitement, until his leg pressed against something that GAVE. He froze. The tiny pressure on his shin was still there. He moved forward slightly, felt the pressure tighten - though it was still only slight. Moving with infinite patience and deliberation he let his hand drift slowly down his leg until the wire was trapped between thumb and forefinger. He swallowed, then allowed himself a grin that would have been feral in appearance if it could have been seen. He'd got them!

He moved to turn and bumped straight into Norm. He cursed. Norm stepped back quickly and collided noisily with a heavily sprung branch. The branch moved with a giant rustling of leaves that wrecked the silence. The three men stood, rock solid. Waiting. Then Finnbar peered ahead, beyond the wire and into the gloom. Nothing. No sound. Taking a cautious breath he unearthed a flashlamp from his jacket and fumbled for the switch. He was taking a chance, and he knew it, but it was the best way he knew to flush out the prey he was hunting. Besides, he confided to himself, he was impatient for the kill. Holding out the flashlamp, he pressed the switch.

The light came on, and for an elongated moment Congreave's face, a face he recognised better than he might have guessed, was caught squarely in the beam. He was frozen in place, eyes wide, mouth gaping, then in an instant he was moving, out of the light and into action. Finnbar felt a roar growing in his chest. Shouldering aside the restraining branches that surrounded him, he charged, screaming: "Hit them!!!"

Colin had been sitting quietly when he felt the first faint pressure on the wire in his hand. He was alert at once, and when the branches rustled he moved into a sprung crouch. When the light jabbed at his eyes he was blinded, momentarily, but had the prescence of mind to move for space. Spots of colour throbbed before his eyes, and his one thought when he heard the cry was that he must buy time for himself, stay free until he could recover from the loss of night vision. He felt his foot thud against something, and knew it was the slowly stirring form of his partner. No time to do anything but shout a warning: "Jack, move!!"

Jack Burt was surfacing instinctively. On a reflex. He was back in the jungle, back in time nearly twenty years, and his platoon was being hit by an NVA night patrol. As he reared upwards, one hand groping for his gun, he sensed more than saw an arm raised in attack, and he blocked the blow with his forearm. The collision shook every fibre of his body and he knew he had been hit with some heavy, clublike object. Still, he forced himself upright, for to fall was to die. He felt an attacker up close in the blackness, raining blows upon him as he struggled for height. Then calculating position he unleashed a mighty punch and felt satisfaction when it connected, forcing a grunt from his attacker and a brief cessation of the attack. He had only moments to evaluate, and what he saw frightened him.

Congreave, starkly outlined in the narrow beam from the flashlamp, was battling mightily with two men, only feet away. Without hesitation Jack leapt in, roped an arm around the neck of one of the men and levered him backwards, forcing him to the ground. Locking his forearm around the man's throat, he *squeezed.*

Now facing only one man, Colin began to parry blows and counter with more success. Then he missed with a kick and went sprawling. The man who leapt on him seemed enveloped in a rabid fury, and Colin knew in his heart that he was locked in deadly combat with Finnbar Craig.

Finn's breath was hot and fetid. He snorted with each exertion. His grimy hands clawed at Colin's face, lacerating clods of flesh from his cheeks, and gouging at his eyes. Colin screamed, and the power of his voice seemed to raise him to greater effort. He fought to rationalise, to analyse his position and that of the man above him, look for a weakness he could exploit. The wire was still in his hand, miraculously still trapped in his clenched fist. But the wire was slack, and he guessed it had snapped. The slackness gave him an idea. As Finnbar's hands closed on his neck and squeezed ever tighter, he fought back the blackening of his senses and looped a length of wire around the Irishman's neck. Taking a length in each hand, he drew a painful breath through his constricted throat and pulled with all the strength he could muster.

At first he thought he had failed; the pressure on his throat seemed to increase. Blood pulsed heavily behind his eyes, and he teetered on the brink of blacking out. But as he maintained the pressure he felt the wire sinking into flesh, compressing muscle, and then the pressure on his throat lessened. Finn was choking, his hands left Colin's throat and clawed at his own neck, fingertips straining to get under the cutting wire.

Colin wanted to cheer; he was winning. He'd hurt him! But he controlled himself. He was not out of the woods yet. Snatching a breath, he yanked on the wire again. Finnbar's attack became a frantic scramble to escape. He wheezed and sputtered, his hands clawing vainly for a grip on the wire. Despite his own pain, Colin was beginning to enjoy the reversed role. In the half light, the looming shadows, he glimpsed the dark contours of Finnbar's face, saw the bulging of his eyes. But so intense was his concentration he did not see another of the men rushing in until it was too late, and a heavy kick to the side of his head hurled his senses into a spin. His hands lost their grip on the wire and he slumped back, helpless.

Jack had recovered quickly from his tussle. He groped for his gun and found it in the grass. Peering hard to single out the Irishmen, he raised the weapon, determined to finish the thing once and for all. Colin was on the ground, and standing over him was a man with a thick stave in his hands. The man raised the stave over his head, intent on delivering a crushing blow. Jack's reaction was pure reflex; he put three bullets into the man's back.

The sound of the gun blasts was enormous. The silence that followed even larger. The man with the stave held his position for what seemed an age, then his hands loosed their grip. The stave fell to the ground and the man crumpled into a heap on top of Congreave.

Jack had been aware of the other two attackers in the clearing. Now he spun, determined to take out at least one more, but they had both gone. He could hear the crashing sounds they made as they charged through the undergrowth. Jack did not relax his guard. While Colin began to recover, Jack circled warily until his reawakened senses told him the danger had, for the moment, receded.

Colin had hauled himself into a sitting position. He ached all over; his throat, his face. He could barely see. Blood was in his eyes. They were on fire! Panic surged, and it took an effort of will to pin it down.

Jack squatted before him. He held up the flashlamp to examine Colin's face. "Jeez, what a mess! That guy scratches like a bitch! Can you see?" He stared aghast at the livid gashes torn in his friend's face, and the trails of blood running dark red in the light.

"Barely," Colin replied. "Clean me up will you? We can't stay here. They'll be back once they've had time to lick their wounds."

Culum followed the sounds of retching to find Finnbar leaning against a tree, bile spattering from his mouth. Culum had a pocket lamp. He ran the beam over Finnbar, saw his deathly white face and the inflamed ring-scar around his neck.

Finn looked at him, and his face, despite it's pain, was contorted into a look of fury. He spat bile. "We showed them, eh, Cully? Give me a few minutes and we'll finish them off."

Culum muttered flatly. "Norm's dead, Finnbar."

Finn stood up straighter. His gaze meeting Culum full on. He looked uncomfortable; things had not gone to plan. "I heard the shots and got the hell out of there. I couldn't breath. It was bad." he paused. "I'm glad you survived old friend. Tis only right we be in at the kill together."

Culum took a deep breath, steeled himself, then plunged in: "Let's go back, Finn. Let's go home. Nothing good can come of this."

At this challenge Finnbar stiffened. The fear, the shock at being beaten back, was banished, and the wild look began to reassert itself. "We've been through a lot together, Cully. I have to know I can count on you." His tone augured danger, but in his eyes shone something different; desperation. The way he saw it, he had gone out on a limb for a man he thought was a friend. Now he feared he might be stranded by that same friend. Culum recognised the symptoms; he knew that Finn was at his most dangerous when cornered. "You are with me, aren't you, Cully?"

Culum knew what he wanted to say. What he ought to say. But he also knew he could not say it - yet. The shift in his own attitudes had him puzzled. All he knew was that since Mary's death his heart had not been in the cause. No, it was more than that. He had learnt not only to question the methods his people - and the Brits in response, used, but he had learnt to be afraid. Really afraid.

But there were still too many things he owed Finnbar. Though his friend had gotten a little crazier each year, a little more dangerous, he had remained loyal to Culum. Loyal and protective. These were hard things to forget. He sighed.

Finn desperately wanted to feel supported. His nerves had

been worsening lately, but he had never been quite this edgy before. Putting out a hand, he took hold of Culum's elbow and steered him forward. "C'mon, let's finish it."

Cleaned up, Colin's wounds did not look so bad, though his sight was still impaired. Now as he sat, gathering his wits to make a move, Jack left him to examine the body of the dead man.

"No ID." he muttered. "But we do know there are only two of them left." He stared around, listened, and then glanced at Colin. "You ready to move?" Colin said he was and Jack helped him to his feet. Supporting him, Jack found it difficult to lift the two backpacks. So dumping them, he ferried Colin to a safe distance before returning. As he stepped back into the clearing to retrieve the packs, he found himself caught in the beam of a flashlamp. He halted, dead still. His mind whirled ideas around. He heard the click of a weapon being cocked. He remained where he was, cold-welded to the spot. His gaze moved and he saw that he was facing a short, stockily built man with dark curly hair and a not unpleasant face. He had a rifle tilted directly at Jack's head. The man slowly lowered the flashlamp to the ground, all the time keeping Jack in the the beam, and the gun trained. The two stared at each other, then the stranger lowered his weapon and made a shooing movement with his hand. Jack was puzzled; he was at the mercy of the killer, yet the man appeared to be warning him off, urging him to run. At that instant a second man appeared through the trees to Jack's right. He took in the situation in a second and cried out as he fumbled for his own rifle. "Kill him Cully! Kill him! Do it!"

Jack turned and ran, delved into the tangle of branches, bellowing a path with wide sweeps of his arms. His legs pumped hard. As he raced he heard a last, impassioned cry, the cry of a beast frustrated at the kill. "CULLEEEE!"

At breakneck speed Jack crashed into the small clearing where Colin was resting. The Englishman had heard the shouts and was up on his feet and ready. Without a word he fell into a stumbling stride alongside Jack, who called out, at the first opportune moment: "I couldn't get the packs. We've lost the food, weapons, everything!" Colin found breath enough to curse aloud. But even as his mind pondered the problems, it was supplying answers. He had lived off the land and in hunted conditions before. He could cope. He and Jack dashed headlong, determined to put distance between themselves and the pursuers. Distance they could convert into time they could use to prepare for the next confrontation.

But they were not being pursued. Not yet. Finn and Culum glared at each other across the clearing, Norm's body sprawled between them like a line of demarcation.

"It's over, Finn." Culum called out bravely, though he felt far from brave. Finn's rifle was aimed straight at his chest, and the muzzle trembled visibly as Finn fought to contain his fury. "We didn't kill Burt's family. We have no right to be hunting him. As for Congreave, him killing Mary, that was business. Part of the cost I agreed to pay when I took up with the cause."

Finn continued to stare. From his expression it was plain the battle raging inside of him was titanic. Culum knew that Finn's instincts would be screaming for a kill, but as he peered into the black single eye of the rifle, Culum knew that he wanted very much to live. Gulping to soothe the dryness in his throat, he quietly offered up a prayer. As they stood for what seemed an age, the early grey mist of daylight began to filter through the trees.

Then Finnbar's internal struggle ended. The old Finn

seemed to emerge triumphant. Though the strain showed, he managed to force a smile to his lips. The rifle was lowered, and Finn heaved a sigh.

"Ah, Cully. You'll be my downfall so you will. But maybe you have a point. I don't like standing out here in the middle of a strange land. Our place is at home, fighting for the cause where we can do the most good, and the most damage to the Brits."

He strolled forward, stepped over Norm's body, dropped the rifle to the ground and moved to accept Culum into his embrace.

Culum felt hot tears rise to his eyes. They misted his vision. It never should have come to this. Finn was a brother, and would be forever. They had fought against the world, there was no need for them to fight each other. He felt Finn's strong arms around him, and then something else, something cold and piercing, struck deep into his lower back and surged upwards. He stiffened, but the pain drove up, and deeper, until it almost lifted him off his feet. Then he saw Finn's face in close-up, saw the evil glee mirrored there, and knew that his friend, his brother, was lost forever. He was dying. Finn was killing him. His long bladed knife wreaking irreversible damage. A whimper fled his lips, the tears turned cold on his cheeks, and he started to sink to the soft earth. There he lay, staring glassily at the receding night, the stars still twinkling.

"Finn...." he whispered weakly.

Then a dark shape loomed, blotting out the stars. Finn placed the tip of the blade squarely over Culum's heart, and leaned down with all his weight.

35:

Leaving Culum's body, Finn began to walk forward. In his mind some new entity - some sinister outside force, had taken control. He seemed to be on the outside looking in.The essential him had been pinned down, trapped, and though he knew he had been wrong to kill his friend, he had been powerless to intervene.

It started to rain. Rain drumming softly on leaves the only sound save his damp trudging. Almost unconsciously he started to pick up the pace. One notch, another. Until he was running, blind to the jagged branches that scored him as he ran. His breathing was rapid but even, his eyes glinted, unseeing through the blackness but perceiving everything. He ran until he was out of the woods, then he stood in the open, arms spread, fists clenched, feet wide apart, head darting as he scoured the landscape. Dawn was approaching, the light softened by the mist of rain. High ground! The thought shrieked in his mind, and he was running once more, pounding the sodden earth as he raced for the top of the nearest hill.

He arrived at the top in a shattered condition, barely able to stand, attaining the plateaued peak on all fours. His chest heaved, and he wheezed like a motheaten bellows. It took long minutes - an age - for him to stand upright. Arms akimbo, he scanned the low and high ground, what he could see of it, sight attuned to the slightest movement on the verdant slopes and valleys. A broad stream snaked between the hills, disappeared between mounds of glistening rocks and reappeared, snaking more awry. He followed it's path until it vanished from sight, then drew back with a gasp as he spotted movement on the nearest hill, perhaps a half mile or so away. Two men, plainly struggling, were hauling themselves towards the crest of the hill. Finnbar growled, angered somehow by their attempts to avoid him. He hurled himself forward a dozen steps, snapped the rifle to his shoulder, took aim, and fired.

The blast echoed eerily, seemed to take an age to fade. In frustration he watched the two small figures crest the hill and plunge out of sight.

His fists shook, and the rifle around which they were clamped shook also. Rain teemed down his face. His dark hair, fringe plastered to his scalp, gave his white face a devilish appearance. He cursed as he realised he would have to get closer. Taking a firming breath, he began to walk down the slope.

To Colin and Jack, the shot rang uncomfortably close. "What now" Shouted Jack. Colin was stumbling ahead, the steepness of the slope the driving impetus. He called back: "We keep going. Once down we should be able to find cover. Behind those rocks." He pointed to a spot, far below, where the stream had reappeared, widened, and run through and over a mass of misshapen rocks, forming pockets of deep, fairly still water, and small, speeding rapids and waterfalls. "They'll have to come after us."

Jack nodded and struggled on. He watched Colin, hurtling ever faster down the slope, and had to admire his guts. The man had all but lost his sight, his eyes badly gashed by Finnbar's tearing fingernails, and he was in considerable pain from the kicks he had received. Jack started to walk faster, the pull of the earth great enough to make him forcibly slow down. The rain still poured, whipped up by the growing wind it fell in great slanting sheets, turning the ground to marsh. The two men slithered down the slope, collapsing into a muddy tangle at the base. Jack helped the almost sightless Colin to his feet. They looked at each other, coated in mud and soaked through, and suddenly began to laugh aloud.

"You think maybe we're running out of luck?" Jack asked, controlling his laughter. Colin shook. "No. We're not finished yet. C'mon. Let's get across the stream."

On leaden legs they trudged as quickly as they could across the increasingly boggy earth.

Finnbar raced up the hill at an unnatural pace. Beyond fatigue, the force now controlling him spurred him unmercifully, intent only on driving him after the prey. He reached the crest of the hill above Colin and Jack before the two men had gotten halfway to the stream. There he stood, drawing deep, triumphant breaths, believing himself the master of all he surveyed, with a power even over the fates. He raised the rifle and fixed a bead on the two indistinct figures outlined against the coarsely grassed plain. The rain pouring down his face forced him to wipe clear his eyes. Muttering incoherently to himself, he aimed, took up the slack on the trigger and fired. The boom echoed enormously in the damped-down silence. The recoil knocked him backwards, but not before he saw one of the figures fall to the ground.

He scrabbled onto all fours and, shielding his eyes with a hand, peered through the drizzling mist. The remaining man was bending over his downed friend.

"Now, you bastid." Finn growled, a mean grin dividing his face. On his feet he began to hurtle down the slope. As if impelled by dark forces he ran down the treacherous hillside, heedless of the slipping stones and mud underfoot. He could not be hurt. He could not fall. He knew it. He was chosen. Darkly shielded from harm he crashed through the mist, the rifle still grasped tightly in his hand.

Then he was on the flat and coming up on his prey.

The man saw him, and for a moment it appeared he almost decided to stay and fight it out. Then he saw the rifle, and ran, tired legs pumping with renewed power.

Finnbar hared in pursuit. Breath came to him in painful snatches and his lungs burned with exertion. His boots struggled on the muddy surface. Then he stopped, lifting the rifle for the final time and took careful aim. His eyebrows tilted in a devilish 'Vee' and his eyes glittered like jet. His lips were drawn back, revealing broken, uncared for teeth, and his tongue hovered, tasting the salt-rain, savouring victory. He pulled the trigger.

Nothing happened. The trigger fell dead. Though the target was clearly outlined in his sights, he could not kill him. The weapon was empty and he cursed himself for not checking.

Hurling aside the weapon he started to run again. Faster and faster he ran, his eyes like knives, aimed unwaveringly on the struggling figure ahead. Faster and faster until he felt he was running faster than any man ever had, and as he hurtled along he drew out his long bladed knife and fixed it firmly in his grasp.

The man ahead had arrived at the stream. He was wading, forcing himself across with the last traces of his strength and reaching the slippery bank. As he scrambled in the mud, hauling himself up the bank, he seemed to come aware of Finn's approach. He shot a sluggish glance over his shoulder. Then Finn was powering in and their gazes locked for the fleetest instant. The prey turned to flee, but his strength had gone. His legs could no longer carry him.

Finn burst across the stream and leapt upon him, and with a growl buried the blade in the man's back. The prey went down, his cheek pressed into the mud, his breath driven from him, while above, Finn withdrew the knife and plunged it again, this time burying it to the hilt. Again and again he sank the blade into the still body until his arm, becoming leaden and weary, gave out. He rolled off the body of his enemy and sat, waist deep, in the rushing stream. The icy water flooded his clothes and numbed his skin, but still he sat there, lungs furiously drawing deep draughts, rain streaming down his face, tongue whipping around his lips leaving flecks of foamy saliva.

As he glanced up it seemed to Finnbar, in his beaten state, that he saw a vision; a giant of a man emerging from the mist. Though wrecked with fatigue his warning instincts still triggered an alarm. He lifted the hand that held the knife and registered, with some surprise, the utter numbness in his fingers. He could not even feel the knife in his grasp. He croaked: "Who...?" Then relief washed over him as the form clarified. "Dominic!"

His dazed mind did not inquire, it seemed perfectly natural that Dominic be there.

The big man grunted a greeting and reached out a hand. As Finn was hoisted from the water he felt lightheaded, seemed to view things from a heightened perspective. He became aware of the redness of Dominic's hair and the massed, tiny jewelled raindrops shimmering in his beard. He saw the grim set mouth, and those blank grey eyes. He had never liked those eyes. On his feet by the stream he stood, swaying slightly, sodden but gratified. "We won, Cully," he whispered. "We did it. Mary....I did it." He swallowed the wave of emotion that rushed to swamp him, and wiped a hand across his face.

He saw the big man studying the body sprawled on the bank. He smiled. "I did it, eh, Dom-boy? Me. I did it."

"Yeah. You did it."

It was at that instant Finn saw the pistol, hanging

loosely in the hand at Dominic's side. "You won't be needin' that," he blurted, voice growing more strident as elation overcame weariness. "I got 'em all."

Dominic slowly altered position. He faced him levelly. "Not all, Finn."

Before the Irishman could react, Seeler had raised the weapon and put a round into Finn's chest. Away from his heart. With a cry he fell to his knees, hand clutched weakly over the wound. His eyes peered in horror at the red seeping between his fingers. He stared up at Dominic, his eyes brimming water, pain on the edge of his tongue, crying for release.

"Why, Dominic? Why are you doing this?" His voice, warped with pain, was high pitched and weak. "Why?"

Seeler told him, then finished him off.

*

Seeler examined the first body, but knew from the positioning of the bullet wound that any hope of life was slim. The body had no pulse. Seeler moved on, crossed the stream and knelt beside the sprawled second figure. The deep black knife wounds bled steadily. Despite the wounds the pulse throbbed quite strongly. Without a thought Seeler turned the man over, and, sparing only a moment to look at the unconscious face, lifted him up.

Cradling the limp figure in his powerful arms, he started to walk. He had a way to go - to PRISM.

Epilogue

He walked along the path of thick cobbles, gaze idly raking the gravestones that bordered it. This place meant something. This was the place, yes. It felt right. Puzzled, he left the path and wandered amongst the graves, searching the names carved on the stones, feeling he knew all the names, yet none of them.

He found a bench and, mindful of his newly healed wounds, carefully lowered himself onto it. He sat with his forearms resting along his thighs. His face was smoothed, he was calm. Eyes level and thoughts on a distant plane.

It began to rain.

Falling, that had been his last recollection. Falling, and the repeated stabbing sensation in his back. Then blackness; a month like that, at first teetering between life and death. At best only dimly awake, only dimly aware of figures bustling effieciently around him, and the comforting prescence who sat calmly beside the bed. Each time he awoke the calm prescence was there to silently reassure him that all would be well. Frustrated and exhausted by pain and lack of sleep, heavily sedated and yet insomniac, he spent the long nights drifting in and out of a haze of amnesia, unable to make sense of the shifting images that taunted him, tumbling gyroscopically just beyond his grasp.

He slowly grew stronger, until he was strong enough to hear the worst and understand the reason for the gnawing frustration. A terrible shock, they told him. His mind suppressing horrors in order to allow his body to heal. It would all come back, they assured him. They told him his name but it meant nothing, and he had raged, banging his fist on the side of the bed in fury until they had tied down his hands.

His entire life was a blank. All he had was his name. But because that name was his sole possesion, he prized it.

He possesed something else, but it was an intangible, and therefore an irritation. The symptoms were easy to recognise, it was the cause that remained an infuriating enigma. Restlessness, the urge to seek and hurt, would spume, and rear almost beyond control, each time he fingered the business card he had found in the pocket of his jacket the day he shrugged off the protests of the doctors and walked out onto the streets.

After wandering aimlessly he had discovered the card and held it out before his amazed gaze. The once sharp edges had been rubbed soft by constant handling, and it was plain except for a scribbled telephone number on one side, and a simple printed word on the other:

PRISM.

Prism, what it meant he had no idea, but some instinct brought to mind the stranger whose prescence by his bed he had found so soothing. The stranger had left the card there to be found, he was sure. It was a key; left there to help him. And so he had dialled the number.

A man had answered. The words they exchanged were cryptic, but the message was passed effectively enough, and the man with the lost memory learned a little about himself; he had a background steeped in intrigue.

Prism. His gut instincts, obviously well developed despite his vacant memory, insisted it meant something vital. He had agreed to the rendezvous because he had to know the meaning and, perhaps, find all the answers.

He was a man used to control, he knew that much from

the patient attitude he had adopted in hospital. To get well he had to rest - so he rested.

The rain felt good. It shone on his lapels, glistened in his hair, tried to chill him but failed. He was strong. His patience had paid off. He was well again and ready to know the answers; Prism.

Rising to his feet, he turned for the cemetary gates at a leisurely stroll and began.

*

A small iron bridge spanned the ornamental stream that dissected the park. He stood in the middle of the bridge, fingers gripping the rail, gaze traversing ceaselessly, watching, but for what? Around a corner of massed trees a family appeared, walking, a young child running playfully ahead. He found himself looking away; the sight of the happy grouping too uncomfortable. There was a choking constriction in his throat.

He heard the patter of feet on the flagged surface of the bridge. He turned on impulse and came to face the child, a small boy.

"Why, it's Ben." he said aloud, surprising himself at the soft exclamation. The boy stared back at him in open wonder.

The rest of the family walked into view. He saw the faces, and suddenly it was all rushing back at him; the past. The sadness, the tears.

Hearing Jack cry out, then the sound of the gunshot on the dawn air. Dragging Jack through the mud until his strength gave out. Fighting his way across the water and dragging himself up a muddy slope. Falling to the ground as the crazed killer plunged the knife into his back.

It was all upon him, and so suddenly, a lump appeared in his throat and tears rose to his eyes. Then they were all together, locked in an emotional embrace. Anne, the kids, all chattering at once, laughter mingled with tears, so much love.

Colin was dimly aware of the prescence standing just outside the group; Seeler. And he knew the big man had been the one at his bedside making sure everything was done for him. His good friend. He thought back to Jack, and Parsons, and Sam, and he felt an immense weight in his heart. Good friends.

They turned to leave, and Colin, holding out his hand, brought Seeler into the group and they were at once all family. There was much to talk about, Colin knew, and there would be pain and sadness, but he was well enough now, strong again. He would take his life into his hands and remake it.

The rain stopped.

*